Fifteen Seconds

Of Normal

Alex Marestaing

MyMilou Press/USA

There's an unfortunate side effect of love,
an infinite ache that keeps us up at night

Thatcher Kelly

1

AFTER THE PICTURE

THATCHER

Thatcher pulled on the T-shirt. It smelled. It was wrinkled. It looked stupid, totally stupid.

He leaned his phone at eye level on the bookshelf, set the timer, and held up the quote.

If everyone isn't beautiful, then no one is.

Andy Warhol. An ironic choice, considering the dude was a pacifist, and the picture Thatcher was about to take was a declaration of war.

The phone clicked, and it was over. At least for now, in the late-night minutes before morning, before the world would see.

He stared at the image and momentarily panicked. Why was he doing this? That school picture had ruined his life, ruined everything. And now he was trying to re-create it?

The answer was difficult and easy all at once. It was Shakespeare, and Dickens, and a million other writers who had inspired him with their words. It was anger, and inspiration, and an insatiable desire to become something better. But mostly, it was Kaeya. The Ghost. The girl who appeared and vanished like a morning mist...the girl he was beginning to love.

KAEYA

Can wishes be made on glow in the dark stars? Yes. Definitely. At least Kaeya thought so, as she stared up at the ceiling and traced make believe constellations with her outstretched finger.

She'd wished upon those stars, endlessly and always, and now one of those wishes had come true. She looked down at the text for the millionth time. It was happening, really happening.

She sat up on her bed and imagined walking into LuLu's on Friday night. The place would be packed and noisy, as always. She'd see him sitting toward the back.

He'd look up and smile, and she'd smile back. And that was as far as she could imagine. Because going on a first date with Kieran Summerlin was a mystery, a blissful mystery, one that gave her nightmares.

Why had she agreed to coffee? Kieran would find out, for sure. LuLu's was small, and he'd be close, close enough to notice what she'd transferred to Glen Canyon High School to hide.

She was terrified, but excited. Mostly excited. Well, maybe mostly terrified. She couldn't really tell due to an extreme case of Kieran-induced insomnia. She liked him, more than liked him, wanted him more than anything she'd ever wanted. And for the first time in forever, she felt confident that a guy—a perfect, *straight out of an H&M ad* looking guy—might actually like her back.

She had Thatcher to thank for that, Instagram Thatcher. Thatcher who'd accidentally stumbled upon her hiding place and discovered her heart, discovered and didn't mind.

2

THE WEEK BEFORE

THATCHER

He hadn't met Kaeya yet, on the day of the picture, the worst day of his life.

It had been a normal morning, full of normal morning things. Until the storm hit, all at once and out of nowhere, like being crushed from behind by a wave while happily waving to your friends on the beach.

He'd been writing a quote in his journal: *They agreed passionately, out of the depths of their tormented lives.* The line was depressing, but Thatcher scribbled it down anyway.

"Seriously, Will. Have you considered antidepressants?" he mumbled as he flipped closed his journal and hopped out of bed.

Of course, Thatcher Kelly knew that William Golding, the one and only author of *Lord of the Flies*, was dead. He was a high school junior and well aware of the logistics of mortality. But he talked to him anyway, out loud even.

No, he didn't believe that Golding was actually listening. But talking to dead authors was an inescapable habit of his, a tribute to the books that had embedded themselves in his soul.

Had Thatcher known how utterly miserable the

day would become, he would have stayed in bed that morning, collecting more beautiful words from more beautiful books, another obsessive habit of his. But his mother was crying when he slugged into the kitchen. Not just crying, sobbing deeply from the little-girl part of her heart. And Thatcher—whose hypersensitive emotions hid behind the bangs of his dirty blond hair—could feel her tears as if they were his own.

He'd seen her cry before, but not like this. Her shoulders heaved, her tears dripped into the dish-piled sink, and the blue veins on her neck bulged as she gripped the edge of the basin.

He knew instantly. It was Dad. His parents had been arguing a lot over the past few months. Always hushed. Always behind photo-lined walls that weren't soundproof enough. And even though their whispered yells were fierce, they'd always emerge smiling like the parents in the perfect family pictures.

Thatcher had always forced himself to believe in those smiles. Until now. Now his mother's pain was out in the open, and he had no idea what to do with it. So he just stood there, frozen to the cold tile floor as he tried to process the sick panic that was rising like an overflowing toilet.

"Drop Scout off on your way to school. Okay?" Mom sniffed as she wiped tears away with the back of her hand. "Leave now or she'll be late."

School? Now? he thought over the chaotic choirs of neurons in his head. Besides the fact that his mother was having seizures at the sink, he hadn't taken a shower, hadn't brushed his teeth, hadn't even looked in the mirror yet.

Thatcher glanced over at his little sister, who was

eating breakfast and playing a game on Mom's phone. She didn't even have her shoes on yet.

"Can't Dad do it?" he argued softly, instantly regretting the words. It was a cruel question, a question he already knew the answer to, but the words were birds locked in a box and flapping furiously. They needed to come out.

More silence, mixed with the fairy-filled soundtrack of Scout's game.

"He's gone," Mom finally answered, stifling back a sob as she pretended to rinse dishes.

Scout shoved another sugar-piled mini pancake in her mouth, completely oblivious to the fact that the Kelly household was crumbling down on top of her curly blond head. But Thatcher knew. He was sixteen, and even though his mother's answer was short and vague, he inferred that she meant Dad was gone, as in *for good*.

"Was it someone, you know...someone else?" he asked cautiously, as if the words were explosives.

Mom broke into another chorus of sobs, and Thatcher knew he was right.

"Someone from work?"

"Enough already!" Mom erupted as she threw a plate into the sink, shattering the glass. "Just give me some space. Okay?"

Startled, Thatcher nodded. He'd never seen her like this. He looked over at his sister, then over at the clock. It was almost eight. Scout's school would be starting in ten minutes. School was normal. She needed normal.

He snatched his car keys off the kitchen counter, grabbed his sister's shoes, and headed out the door. Without taking a shower. Without brushing his teeth. Without changing out of the T-shirt and sweats he had slept in. Because Mom was still sobbing. Because his little sister was late. Because his father had ditched them, and he didn't want to be anything like him.

KAEYA

Kaeya didn't know Thatcher, not really. Oh, she knew he was in one of her classes, third-period history, but she hadn't talked to him or anything. She thought he dressed cool, like a European, but that was about it.

In other words, Thatcher Kelly wasn't really on the radar that morning, the morning of the meme. Not at all. She had other things to worry about, like the fact that she was on her fourth outfit: faded brown combat boots, another vintage skirt, her favorite white T-shirt—the thrift-shop miracle—and a scarf to bring it all together.

It wasn't perfect, no outfit ever was. But was it perfect enough?

She had to decide. Now. School was starting in a little over thirty minutes. Usually that would have given her plenty of time. But not today. It was picture day—her first ever at Glen Canyon High—and if she didn't get there early, the lines would grow to Disneyland lengths.

Since transferring to Glen three weeks earlier, Kaeya had tried to avoid crowds, as much as that was possible in a school of four thousand. It was a critical part of her plan, a plan that was working, and she didn't want to mess it up.

"Looking good," her dad called from the hallway as he dashed by. He was her biggest fan and only roommate in a house that had grown way too empty after the death of her mother three years earlier.

"Not really," Kaeya mumbled as she looked down at her legs for the millionth time. They were too pale for California, and the skirt showed too much of them. Yeah, she definitely needed to change.

Dad heard. He was back. "You calling me a liar?" he said as he straightened his purple tie.

"Not a liar, just fashion challenged." She smiled as she ducked back into her walk-in closet.

"Hey, I'm hip. I'm groovin'," he joked as he did a little dance in the doorway.

"Says the man with the purple and polka-dotted tie," she called as she emerged with a handful of shirts.

"Okay, how about this? I'll ditch the tie if you stop obsessing about your outfit."

Kaeya appreciated the love, but if she was going to make this whole school-transfer thing work, she'd have to rely on her own opinions this time around, not the opinions of school psychologists, or well-meaning teachers, or even her own father. So no, the skirt wouldn't do. And that meant the brown boots weren't going to work either.

"Dad, I love you. Now leave," she said as she battled with her bootlaces. Her father wanted to help. She could tell by the *You'll always be my little girl* look in his eyes, but she wasn't going to let him. Kaeya could untie her own shoes, even when her hands and neck twitched and her fingers balled up into fists. It would just take longer.

When she finally finished, she looked up again. He was still there, standing in the doorframe. "Kaeya, why are you doing this to yourself? Just go back to

Centennial," he pleaded, his thick Argentinean accent easily understandable to the daughter who'd been hearing it for sixteen years. "Everyone knows you there."

She pinched the bridge of her nose and shook her head. "Dad, can we please not have this conversation right now?"

Kaeya's father hardly ever frustrated her. They got along, like two struggling sailors working to keep their leaky little boat afloat. But he was frustrating her now because they'd had the same sorry conversation every single morning since she'd changed schools. No, she wasn't going back to her old high school. Never. Ever. Not even if they paid her in piles of Forever 21 gift cards. The end.

Her father was silent. He felt bad for bringing the topic up. She could tell by the way he was running his hands through his receding black hair. Though he didn't agree with the transfer to Glen Canyon, he knew how important it was to her, and that was enough.

"Kaeya, remember. Paint your heart right..."

"I know. I know," she said as she struggled with the boot. "And your makeup won't matter."

The words were Mom's, Kaeya's wise and beautiful best friend. Unlike her father, Mom would have understood that the subtle but painstakingly applied makeup and piles of rejected outfits on the floor were only distractions, masks to hide what was really going on. Especially today. Picture day. The day when she had to stare into a camera and smile like the day was normal.

The day when an entire line of students would be watching...a line that might notice.

THATCHER

Had he known that he was driving toward Kaeya, mere minutes away from first contact, the morning would have been at least bearable. But, of course, he had no clue. So dropping his lonely little sister off at the kindergarten gate was utterly depressing.

"Want me to walk you to your line?" Thatcher asked as he grabbed Scout's Care Bears lunch bag off the backseat and handed it to her. She took it and shook her head no.

On the way to school, his sister had talked nonstop about how they were going to watch some video in class, something about Chinese dragons. But now that Thatcher had pulled up to the curb, she'd stopped talking altogether.

"Well, you better be going then, okay?"

Scout nodded slightly but didn't budge, so Thatcher gently unbuckled her seat belt and reached over to open the passenger side door. It worked. Scout dropped her legs over the side of the seat and started to leave. But before her toes touched pavement, she turned and hugged him with a long, hang-on-for-life hug. And he hugged her back, just as tight, because she needed it. And so did he. And they would both need each other's hugs again and again in the next few days and months and years. Thatcher was certain of this.

He watched as his sister walked up to a group of girls, all perfectly dressed in mall-bought clothes and giggling near the flagpole. They all smiled as she approached, but Scout, dressed in the same Hello Kitty T-shirt and shorts she'd worn to bed, didn't smile back. The missing smile left him with an empty feeling as he pulled out of the school's parking lot and past the kindergarten playground, the playground that made him feel old.

KAEYA

Kaeya hadn't planned on crashing into Thatcher either. But he happened to be at the right place at the right time, a solitary scrap of wood in a stormy sea when she'd needed something to cling to.

Surprisingly, she'd reached school early, something she didn't like, because it gave her too much time to think. With a few minutes to kill, she reached into the glove compartment and pulled out the bottle of pills, Haldol this time, one of the many meds on an endless carousel prescribed by a doctor who seemed to be guessing half the time.

She hated the way the way it made her feel all sluggish and gray. Besides, meds never really helped anyway. Tossing the unopened bottle of pills into the glove compartment, she took one final look in the mirror. Her straight, shoulder-length black hair looked fine. Her blush subtle.

You can do this, she thought, reminding herself that yesterday she'd lasted over an hour before the beast arrived, a new record. Today, her goal was to last even longer.

Kaeya looked down at her bracelet watch. She had time. So with a deep breath, she turned on the radio and sank back into her seat. Music always helped.

THATCHER

The song on the radio was a mistake. Coldplay. "The Scientist." It made him think. About Dad leaving and Mom crying. About the time ages ago when Dad squirted Mom with the hose and how Scout had giggled, and how things like that would probably never happen again.

Then came the tears, from the back of his eyes like a pipe had burst in his brain. And in a matter of seconds, the tears morphed into sobs, fierce toddler-like heaves that shook his shoulders as he drove.

KAEYA

The song on the radio was a mistake. Coldplay. "The Scientist." She stayed away from depressing songs before school. They made her feel too much, and emotions before school were annoying, like mosquitoes.

She turned the radio off. It was time to go anyway.

THATCHER

By the time Thatcher pulled into the school parking lot, his eyes were red and his nose a fountain. Definitely not okay.

Cracking open the car door, he squirted his water

bottle on his face and wiped his eyes. But one look in his rearview mirror told him it was a lost cause. He looked like a nightmare.

Ditching class was the only option. He started the car, jammed it into reverse, then shut the engine off. He couldn't leave. His mom would freak. Totally freak.

With no other option, he got out of the car, buried his head in the hood of his gray sweatshirt, and marched toward first period, ignoring the feeling that every step was a mistake.

KAEYA

The usual group of guys sat in their usual spot near the front steps, playing some medieval-looking card game, lost in their quests, hidden behind long hair, glasses, and trench coats. She'd heard them talking about her once, about how she looked exactly like the elven princess Arwen from *The Lord of the Rings*. She'd never seen that movie.

"Looking good, Sam," she called to one of them—a bow-tie-sporting Asian guy, the only one who seemed remotely aware that it was picture day. He instantly looked down.

"Um, thanks," he mumbled as Kaeya moved past. When she reached the steps, she heard someone coming up to her from behind. She turned to look. It was Quentin, the ginger-headed and joyful junior that sat near her in AP calculus.

"Hey K," he said as he fell in step beside her. He was panting, like he'd worked hard to catch up. "You didn't show last night."

"Yeah, I'm just not into the whole group-study thing." She smiled as she continued to move forward. "But thanks for the invite."

She felt guilty for not coming to his AP test meet up. She liked Quentin. Everyone liked him. The *way too huge for high school* soccer player had a way of making everyone laugh, even teachers, and she gravitated toward people with a sense of humor. But she couldn't risk a study session, or party, or anywhere where people might get close enough to notice her fatal flaw, the one that constantly threatened to rise to the surface.

Of course, she'd eventually have to increase her social availability. That was part of the whole changing-schools plan. But not yet. For now, social life at Glen would have to be measured, taken slowly in small gulps, with every second savored.

After making small talk about how hard the calc homework was, they headed their separate ways, and the conversation seemed over. But then, when Quentin was about twenty feet away, he turned.

"Kieran was there."

Kaeya blushed at the sound of his name. Third-period Kieran. Blond-haired and gentle and perfect Kieran, who'd instantly made her feel welcome on her first day by leading her to her next class. Why was Quentin mentioning him? Had she been that obvious?

Quentin was singing a Beatles song as he walked away, something about a girl in love. She wanted him to stop, as if her most precious secret had fallen into enemy hands and was now being Wikileaked all over the world. And at the same time, she wanted him to keep on singing. Louder.

Dying of embarrassment, she made a beeline toward the gym, where a group of stressed-out-looking parent helpers were manning picture-day tables. She tried to forget Quentin's comment. It was making her nervous, and stress only made her condition worse. But ignoring Kieran was hard to do, and so it came.

The scowl. The involuntary twitch that made her look like she was sucking on a lemon. Soon there would be more scowls, followed by uncontrollable yells. They'd echo off the gym walls, making people stare, and laugh, and delete her name from future friendships.

She grabbed hold of one of the rubber bands on her wrist and snapped it as hard as she could, a lion tamer cracking the whip. Though Dr. Jaya, her old school psychologist, had told her it was impossible, she would beat this thing back, without help, for as long as was humanly possible.

THATCHER

In an age of iPhones, no one looks up, he thought as he pushed forward into the abyss.

His eyes were still red and his hair a mess, but the words, plucked from a Nadira Salim essay, steadied his feet. No one would notice. He was an introvert, so flying under the social radar would be easy. Right?No. Wrong. So wrong. A million times wrong.

Of course, Thatcher could have survived with his invisibility intact...if it hadn't been for that parent volunteer. She called out to him as he walked past the gym.

"Name please," the woman ordered as he zipped past the fold-up table she was sitting behind.

"W-what?" he asked as he turned to face her.

The woman looked annoyed, even though he'd done nothing but walk by.

"Last name please," she barked as she tapped her pencil on the clipboard she was holding like a weapon.

"Thatcher?" he answered obediently, having no idea why this woman had planted herself on campus.

"I said *last* name," she scolded.

"Oh...Kelly," he stammered, still oblivious.

"Take the ticket to camera number one," she said as she handed him a small numbered paper.

And that was when he realized. They were going to document this nightmare of a morning, in the form of a school picture.

KAEYA

The progression was predictable. First, her mouth would contort. Then, her neck would snap back repeatedly like a crazed bobble head. Finally, she would vocalize, blurt out some random sound, one that would instantly set her apart. She needed another distraction. Fast.

Scanning the gym, she looked for someone she recognized. Neyma! From first period. She was standing in line at the far end of the gym, texting someone on her cell. Perfect. The girl loved talking.

Ditching her place in line, Kaeya raced across the floor. "Hey, Neyma," she called as she casually slipped next to her.

"Hey, K." Neyma smiled, barely looking up from her phone.

"So do you think that...HA! HA!"

The vocalizations had arrived, the part of the disability Kaeya dreaded most. She pretended to cough.

Neyma looked up. "Are you, like, okay?"

"Yeah, it's just...Ha!...something in my throat." It was a fallback answer, one she'd used repeatedly since arriving at Glen. Kaeya laughed and moved on. "So do you think that they'll give us a tardy pass if we're late?"

"Yeah, that's what they did last year," Neyma answered, putting away her phone. "I mean, I'd rather be here than in econ any day. I can barely stay awake in there. Mr. Neil talks sooooo slow."

"I know. Right?"

As Neyma launched into one of her one-sided conversations, Kaeya could feel herself calming down. She didn't need to run. Not yet. As long as she kept listening, focusing on the words, pretending, she could get through.

THATCHER

He liked to think that his Spidey senses had alerted him to the moment, that he'd known somehow that she was there, inches away, and that this first contact was meant to be. But in reality, he'd been too focused on hiding under the hood of his sweatshirt to sense anything.

Just take the stupid picture already, he thought as the sloth-like photographer fiddled with the angle of someone's head. Class was about to start, and his face was a mess, and the last thing he wanted was to have to walk in late and have everyone stare.

Then, as the line crawled forward, he smelled them. Violets. He knew the scent by heart. The new girl. US history. Third row. Second seat. He'd savor the smell of her perfume as she brushed by his desk each day on the way to her desk.

Of course, he'd never spoken a word to her because actually *talking* to her was impossible math. She was just too stunning. And he was just too shy. She was standing directly behind him now. He could tell by the sound of her jangling bracelets. He tried to look forward to avoid her gaze, but she was a magnet, a mysterious magnet that somehow pulled him sideways so that he could see. Her flowery black skirt and khaki green jacket. The French words scrawled across her white T-shirt. Her subtle makeup and shoulder-length black hair.

He knew her name, Kaeya. But in his daydreams he called her Ghost—Ghost because of her paper-pale skin. And Ghost because she was a mystery, always disappearing—in the middle of lectures and presentations and even tests. And for some reason, Mr. Selznick, who was manic about students not missing class, never seemed to mind.

Thatcher tapped his foot nervously against the shiny wood floor. He was a physical and emotional mess. Definitely not the first impression he wanted to make.

Don't talk to me. Don't talk to me, he thought as an overdressed freshman girl bogged down the line by insisting that her picture be retaken.

After an awkward minute or so, the line moved up again, and Thatcher could hear Ghost talking...to someone else.

Relief.

KAEYA

"I had this bizarre dream last night," said Kaeya as she paced forward on the gym floor.

"Not as bizarre as Karaoke with Kyle's parents," said Neyma as she craned her neck to see why the picture line wasn't moving. "Sorry. Go on."

"So I'm walking down this long sidewalk, eating an ice cream cone, cookies and cream I think, when Ernest Hemingway suddenly shows up in a white suit. I recognize him because he's on the cover of my AP Lang book, and I know it must have been during his Cuban phase, because he's ranting about the revolution. I should be shocked, but I'm not, and I just keep on walking past him, completely unfazed, as if talking with Hemingway is the most normal thing in the world."

THATCHER

Hemingway? The Ghost knew Hemingway? Thatcher loved Hemingway. He had nearly fifty of the guy's quotes in his journal.

Though we haven't officially met, perhaps our souls have, he thought, in words straight from *Beauty From Ashes.*

Another book, another quote, like the ones that came to him all the time, as if they were magic and meant something. Today, he hoped so.

KAEYA

"Hemingway?" Neyma interrupted. "Is he a YouTuber?"

She was joking, of course, and Kaeya smiled.

"No, an author. A famous one."

"Oooh, Kaeya's crushing on an author."

"Um, let me see. Seventy years old? White beard? Not my type," Kaeya joked. "Plus, he's dead."

"So who *is* your type?"

Kaeya looked around as if she was about to divulge a deep secret. "Kieran Summerlin," she whispered with conviction. "Definitely."

"Kieran? Are you kidding me?" Neyma teased as she shook her head disapprovingly. "But he's so...so perfect and athletic and sweet to everyone. I have no idea what you see in him."

Neyma laughed at her own sarcasm, something she did a lot. Kaeya would have laughed too, had she not felt another tic coming on. She tensed her face to stop it, but the twitch came anyway, in the form of a silent scowl.

Luckily, Neyma, who was now checking a text, didn't even notice. "Hey look," she said. "This is taking way too long. I'm coming back at lunch."

"Sure," Kaeya answered as her friend turned and left.

Now that Neyma was gone, the tics were threatening to get worse. She needed to talk to someone else. Anyone else.

And there he was. Thatcher Kelly. Whether he liked it or not, Kaeya Garay was about to come crashing in.

THATCHER

A sick reality snapped him out of a Ghost-induced daze. While his picture was being taken, she'd see him, without his hood on, staring lamely into the camera with bloodshot eyes. He needed to get out of line. Now.

But it was too late. Because Ghost was talking...to him.

"Ready for the quiz today?" she asked.

The shock of actually hearing her voice nearly sent Thatcher into a panic attack.

"Um, yeah. I think so," he muttered, his faced glued in the forward position.

"Okay then, what's the first permanent British settlement in North America?"

Before he could answer, the photographer called from beyond the screen. Salvation.

"It's...um...my turn," he squeaked as he pointed toward the screen.

The Ghost nodded as he made a beeline for the picture stool.

Just get this over with, he thought as he stared at the lens.

"No hoods," scolded the irritated photographer, a frazzled-looking middle-aged guy whose monk-like bald spot glistened with sweat.

"Oh, um, sorry," Thatcher said as he reluctantly pulled it off.

The photographer moved back to his camera and stared for what seemed like an eternity. Then, with a disturbed look on his face, marched back to the stool, grabbed Thatcher's head, and tilted it in some unnatural position.

"Your sweatshirt's blending in with the background too much," he said. "You'll have to take it off."

Thatcher had no idea which T-shirt he was wearing underneath his sweatshirt. All he knew was that he'd worn it to bed. And now Kaeya, who was at the front of the line, staring at the scene, would be seeing it in all its wrinkled glory.

He hesitated, but the guy was just standing there with his arms crossed. He had no choice. He pulled the thing off and threw it on the floor.

"Can you please just take the picture?"

"So who died this morning?" joked the photographer as he fiddled with the tripod.

It was a sick joke. Sick because, metaphorically, *Thatcher* was the one dying, right there in front of the entire student body. But he didn't say anything because of Ghost. She was watching. He could feel her eyes.

After a long minute or so, the camera flashed. It was finally over. Thatcher leapt to his feet, pulled on his sweatshirt, and shot to the exit.

"Hey! Don't forget your proof!" the photographer called.

Thatcher turned around and caught Ghost's eyes.

He'd never noticed how blue they were, like a clear sky after a storm. Embarrassed, he stepped back toward the photographer, grabbed the print, and left.

She saw me, he thought as he made his way across the gym. But what did she see? There was only one way to find out. The proof.

Once outside, he glanced at the image. It was awful, as in *Walking Dead* awful. His hair looked like it had undergone shock treatment, and he had this pitiful about-to-cry expression on his face.

And then he noticed. His T-shirt. His stupid Martha Baines T-shirt! The country-singing diva was blowing a kiss toward the camera with the words *My Kind of Guy* in pink cursive scrawled over her head.

Thatcher didn't even like Martha Baines or country music. The shirt was a joke gift from his cousin. He'd only worn it to bed because his mom hadn't done laundry in a while. And now he'd taken a picture in it, the worst picture in the history of school pictures. And he'd taken it in front of Kaeya.

Thatcher tossed the picture in the nearest trash can like it was radioactive. But he should have torn it up first. Because a toxic photo, like toxic waste, needed to be disposed of properly.

KAEYA

Even though math had never been her favorite subject, it was her favorite part of the day, because of Kieran.

She could see him through the open door. He was sitting on a desk and laughing softly as Quentin and some other kids passed around a small strip of paper.

He smiled as she walked in, his blue eyes bright and welcoming. Was the smile for her? She doubted it. It was probably just a leftover laugh from whatever it was he'd been laughing about a few seconds earlier.

"Hey, Kaeya," Kieran said sweetly as she purposely parked herself in the seat in front of him.

"Hey. What's that?" she asked, wondering what was so funny. It looked like one of the picture-day proofs students were given in the gym that morning.

"Oh, this?" Kieran said as he handed the picture back to Quentin. "It's nothing."

Kaeya looked over at Quentin, whose shoulders were heaving as he tried to suppress his laughter. It was definitely *something*, but she was too new to ask to be let in on the joke, so she turned around and waited for Mrs. Candele to arrive.

As the tardy bell rang, her thoughts were interrupted by a tap on the shoulder. She looked back.

"Don't move," Kieran whispered gently as he took hold of the chain around her neck. "Your necklace is stuck in your hair."

If it were anyone else messing with her hair, weird. But Kieran? Completely acceptable. It *was* stuck, and Kaeya didn't mind. Not at all.

"Yeah, it does that sometimes," she said as she pulled on the chain to help. She could feel her fingers touching his for the first time, and the sensation felt fresh and new, like a rain-washed morning.

"Don't pull so hard." He laughed. "You'll break it."

"Okay then, Mr. Jewelry Expert. I'll let you handle it on your own."

As he tugged and pulled, the inevitable happened. Her face started to contort. Kaeya bit her lip. The tics were back, threatening to destroy the moment.

Suddenly, a strange *HA* sound leapt from her throat, followed almost simultaneously by a fake sneeze used to mask it. "*HA...ch!*"

"Sorry!" she added as she wiped her nose with the back of her index finger, an added effect. The leg kicking at age twelve. The crashing into walls at age thirteen. She was used to these unwanted interruptions and a pro at deflecting them.

"That's all right," he said as he gave the necklace another tug. It hurt this time, but she wasn't about to say anything. She would have let him cut off her arm if necessary.

"Try unlatching it," she told him as she snapped her rubber bands in a futile attempt to keep the next tic away. "That...*HA-ch!*...usually works."

"Are you sick?"

"No, just allergic to calculus," she kidded. Yes, it was stupid, dumb, right out of a Disney Channel show. But what else was she supposed to say? She didn't want to lie to Kieran about having a cold. She didn't want to lie to Kieran about anything. Ever.

"One more twist and...got it!" Kieran beamed as he held the silver necklace up and swept a loose strand of her hair back into place.

"Yay!" she cheered, reaching for the necklace. The tics were starting to get bad. She needed to leave. Now. But Kieran wasn't handing the necklace back.

"Th-that's my mom's...*HA-ch*," she said as he looked at the tiny photo inside. For anyone else, this would have been an invasion of privacy. But, again, this was Kieran. And he had an automatic backstage pass to her heart.

He looked up, then back down at the open locket. "She has your eyes," he said as he handed the necklace back.

Kaeya put her head down, hoping beyond hope that she could gain control again. Because she wanted to tell him more. About how the locket was a gift from her mom on their last Christmas together. About the cancer, and how during the entire two years that her mother was sick, it never really dawned on her that her mom and best friend in the world might die, until that rainy Tuesday when she came home from school and the bed was empty. The day the tearing down began. The demolition of her childhood.

Kieran reached for her wrist. "Is something wrong?" he asked as she lifted her head off the desk. He was staring, and his caring, blue eyes made her want to cry.

"HA!"—*cough*—"I'm fine," she said as she held up the locket and stood. "Thanks for the help...with this."

Kaeya pointed at her neck and began backing out of the room. "It's just this throat thing... I'll be fine."She burst into the hall and let out a silent scream. One day she'd tell him, when they were close enough to share the ugly things and love each other in spite of them.

I HAVE TOURETTE'S!

3

TUESDAY

THATCHER

During breakfast, the phone rang while Thatcher poured cereal into a red plastic bowl. It was Dad. He could tell from Mom's tone as she picked up—giddy but trying not to show it, like a freshman being asked on a first date.

When he was done pouring the milk, he moved to the far end of the table to be closer to the action.

In a matter of seconds, Mom's voice grew tense, and she left the room.

Scout looked up from her Fruit Loops.

"Did you hear there's a new Pixar movie coming out?" Thatcher said, pointing to the open newspaper on the table in an attempt to distract her.

"But you bought that truck. Not me." Mom's voice quivered from the living room.

"Have you seen the trailer? It looks pretty good," Thatcher said as he walked over to the sink and turned on the faucet.

"No. There's no way I'm making *your* car payment! And no, I'm not being unreasonable," Mom argued. She was holding her ground, but Thatcher knew it wouldn't last. Dad would say something to make her crumble. He always did.

Mom was screaming now and crying, as Scout, who had left her place at the table and was now standing at the threshold between the kitchen and living room, looked on.

Thatcher picked up his backpack and hurried his sister out the door. He didn't want her to see this version of Mom, the version that was now laying in the fetal position on the sofa, like a wounded boxer.

A ray of sunlight met them in the driveway, the first of the morning, and Scout raised her arms and basked in its warmth. It would be another typical fall day, with neighbors walking dogs and kids playing basketball on the street after school. And for some reason, it dawned on him that the planet didn't really care about the tearing apart of the Kelly home. Not at all.

The thought lingered like a stale odor until his sister broke the silence. "You look good," she said as she happily slid into the passenger seat and buckled her seat belt.

"W-what?" asked Thatcher.

"Your hair and stuff. It looks good."

"Thanks," he said as he started the car. She'd noticed the hair, the gelled and purposely messed up hair he'd spent almost ten minutes on that morning in an obsessive attempt to compensate for yesterday's disaster.

"Did you make it all nice for a girl?" she asked.

"Umm, maybe?" he answered sheepishly as he pulled out of the driveway and onto Narrows Lane.

He wasn't really trying to be funny, but Scout's face bloomed into a huge kindergarten smile, which made Thatcher smile, and then they smiled about that and all sorts of randomness all the way to Scout's school. And when his sister skipped up the school steps towards her clump of tiny friends, he couldn't help but smile again. Because he was suddenly aware of the fact that there was still something left, a tiny remnant of family to float on through the flood.

KAEYA

She noticed the poster by accident, in a passing glance as she turned the corner, like it was magic and meant to be. It showed a sea of Chinese lanterns floating up into a night sky.

Light the Night
Lanterns
October 17th

From what she'd heard, Lanterns was prom, homecoming, and Sadie Hawkins all put together. Some long-retired physics teacher had started the dance back in the sixties as a science project. Students would build their own Chinese lanterns and test them out on the lake. If they flew, they'd get an A. Eventually, the science project morphed into a school dance, and a Glen Canyon tradition was born. After a few decades—and a couple of brush fires—Lanterns was still going strong, minus the flying lantern part.

Kaeya imagined what it would be like. Hiking up to Wisteria Lake in the moonlight and dancing under stars and tree-strung lights. Floating paper lamps on the lake's emerald waters while couples kissed and swayed to the sound of old-school singers like Louis Armstrong and

Frank Sinatra. It sounded perfectly romantic...and
perfectly impossible.

There was just no way she could last that long at
a dance without people noticing. She had a neurological
disorder, an obvious one. Sure, some people had more
severe cases of Tourette's than she did. But hers was bad
enough, and no matter how hard she tried to hide it, her
body would eventually scream, *You don't belong!*

THATCHER

Thatcher made his way down the hall towards freedom.
Algebra 2 was over, and he was looking forward to ten
uninterrupted minutes of *Anna Karenina*. He'd just
started Tolstoy's thousand-page journey, and he was
thirsty for more. If he read quickly, he might even have
time to copy some lines down in his journal.

But before Thatcher could make his escape, Max,
a friend since first grade, grabbed the strap of Thatcher's
backpack and spun him over to a wall of lockers.

"Dude. Look," Max whispered as he motioned
toward the end of the hall. "They're checking you out."

A cute blonde was chatting with a tall, dark-
haired girl. Thatcher recognized them, from sixth-period
Spanish.

"Yeah, right," mumbled Thatcher as he tried to
spin free. But Max—who compensated for his junior high
looks by obsessively working out—wouldn't let go.

"Seriously, dude. They are!" Max was frantically pointing now, way too obviously, considering the girls were only feet away.

Thatcher turned. Max was right. They were staring, subtly, from the corners of deer-oval eyes. "See?" beamed Max while punching Thatcher in the shoulder with his fist.

The tall girl, who looked like a junior or senior, smiled and whispered something into the blonde's ear. And that was when Thatcher noticed. The girls weren't flirting. They were laughing. At him.

KAEYA

Quentin laughed as he shoved his cell phone in her face. "Check this out." She was on her way to the forest biome to study, but apparently that would have to wait.

She grabbed the phone from his hands and took a look. It was a meme, one of those random pictures that fly around the Internet like bugs, pictures that Kaeya usually thought were funny. But this one was different.

The guy in the picture looked like a mess, with hair like Einstein's on a bad day and eyes that were all puffy and red. A caption read: *My hamster and only chess partner died,* SO *MARRY ME MARTHA!*

"Marry Me Martha. Get it?" Quentin laughed. "He's wearing a Martha Baines T-shirt."

Kaeya was supposed to laugh, but she couldn't. Because she recognized the guy in the picture. Thatcher. And as she stared at the meme on Quentin's phone, she wondered. She'd been with him on picture day. How come she hadn't noticed he'd been crying?

THATCHER

By the time he'd escaped Max's clutches, it was way too late to even touch Tolstoy or his journal. But as he pushed his way through the crowds, he saw something that stopped him in his tracks.

Ghost. She was sitting on the edge of a planter, her black hair propped perfectly on her shoulders, her blue eyes smiling as she poured over notes of some kind.

He wanted to keep moving, to escape from the nerves now drop-kicking his stomach. But at the same time, he wanted to explain that the crazy-haired, puffy-eyed guy she talked to at picture day was an anomaly, a small scratch in an otherwise charming personality.

Frozen on the walkway, he obsessed about what to do, until a rare and distant feeling rose up in his chest. Courage. Taking a deep breath, he turned.

"S-so how's Hemingway doing?" he asked while staring at her bracelet-covered ankle.

"Excuse me?" she said, looking more than a little upset.

Five seconds into the conversation and he'd already blown it.

"You were talking about this dream you had," he explained, "on picture day. Remember? The one about Ernest Hemingway, and..."

"Well, yeah, of course I remember. It was *my* dream. But how is it that *you* remember?"

Thatcher's heart raced. He'd stepped over some invisible boundary, and he had no idea how to get back.

"I know how you know," Ghost continued. "You were eavesdropping on a private conversation I was having with a friend. That's how."

"Look, I'm so sorry," he mumbled as he raised his hands in surrender and turned to leave.

But he hadn't moved five feet before he heard her voice again.

"Thatcher! Wait!" She laughed.

His heart practically stopped. "Yeah?" he answered, bracing himself for a tongue-lashing as he turned around.

"I'm just messing with you," she said with a silly grin on her face.

Relief. Joy. She was joking. And she knew his name.

"Okay, so you just totally freaked me out," he said as he cautiously stepped back toward her.

"I'm so sorry. I have this compulsively sick sense of humor." She was laughing at her own joke. Cute.

"That's okay. I mean, I'm just glad you're not ticked off."

Ghost laughed some more, then turned her attention toward the worn-out journal he was carrying. "Ooh, a diary," she mentioned happily as she pointed toward his arm. "Do you write about all your wild crushes in there?"

Thatcher turned red. "Yeah, I guess. If you consider being in love with words a crush."

Ghost raised an eyebrow.

"It's not really a diary," he explained, carefully, so as not to scare her away with his strange literary compulsions. "I collect lines, from books and stuff."

"Lines? About what?"

"I don't know. It depends. Sometimes lines that mean something, sometimes lines that just sound good. Just lines."

"So read me one of these...*lines.*"

"Uh, I don't really..." Thatcher stammered as he took a step back.

"Oh, come on. Just one," she begged.

Her bold, and borderline rude, intrusiveness was attractive, like a well-placed freckle. He couldn't help but give in to her gravity-like pull.

Flipping the journal open, he stared at the words he'd scribbled the night before. "So, um, this is from a book I started reading last night," he stammered as Kaeya stared. He kicked the ground with his toe and sighed, thinking he would tell her he couldn't or shouldn't or didn't want to, but instead he heard his voice say, "'All unhappy families are alike; each unhappy family is unhappy in its own way.'"

"Tolstoy," she said reverently. She looked at the sky a moment, as if to savor the words, then began packing her things in her canvas book bag.

"Um, yeah. *Anna Karenina*," he said, shocked that she knew the line.

She stood and brushed off her skirt. "You've surprised me, Thatcher Kelly."

"I know. Tolstoy. It's weird."

"Not weird. Unique," she objected. "Not a lot of guys are into dead Russian authors."

She even knew Tolstoy was Russian? No way. He wanted to ask *how* and *why* and *when*, but then the third-period bell rang.

"I'm Kaeya, by the way," she said, turning to go.

"Y-yeah, I know," he stuttered as he watched her disappear down the crowded walkway. When he could no longer see her, he closed his eyes and archived the moment. Her eyes. Her scent. Violets. Always violets. He was crushing, too soon, and it hurt.

KAEYA

Mrs. Crandall had given them time to work on homework, but Kaeya couldn't concentrate. Her thoughts were on Thatcher and the conversation they'd just had. She hoped she hadn't scared him away with her little Hemingway joke. The poor guy had enough to worry about with that meme going around, the meme that Quentin was now sharing with the girl in front of him, the girl who passed the phone to the tall guy with the fro, the guy who then passed it to Kaylie Smythe.

As she watched the scene unfold, Kaeya wondered if Thatcher knew. If he didn't know yet, he definitely would soon, because people were asking Quentin to text it to them. And he was.

The crucifixion of Thatcher Kelly had begun, and she had no intention of watching. She got up and left.

Thatcher

Thatcher stared at the book on his desk, the book that Kaeya had touched. Now even Tolstoy was a melancholy reminder of an out-of-reach dream.

He'd felt the sting of infatuation before, lots of times, but never like this. With one word, Hemingway, Kaeya had inadvertently wiggled her way in, and now she was stuck there like a sweet splinter.

Thatcher would have checked out of language arts entirely if it wasn't for the group of guys in the back. They were completely ignoring Mrs. Breslin's lecture and watching him, just like the girls in the hall had done that morning. Their stares were discreet, quick glances between whispers, but they were obvious enough for him to notice.

Whenever Thatcher turned around, they would practically jump back into their note taking, acting as if they were deeply fascinated by the list of transitive verbs on the board. But when he turned back, he could hear muffled laughter, secret and shared.

Something was wrong with his face or his clothes or something. The worst part was that Kaeya might have noticed when they'd spoken earlier.

That last thought sent him into a panic. He needed a mirror. Now. So as calmly as possible, he stumbled toward the hook where Mrs. Breslin hung the hall pass and sauntered out of the room. Once the door was closed, he frantically ran down the empty halls and into the bathroom.

The fluorescent lights were bare and bright, leaving no facial imperfection to the imagination. He looked at his face, then looked again. Nothing. No zits dying to burst, no food on his chin, no Scout-drawn permanent-marker mustache on his upper lip.

Next, he backed away from the mirror to inspect the rest of his body, but there was nothing. No open zipper on his skinny jeans. No stains on his V-neck T-shirt. No embarrassing rips anywhere.

"So *what* is it?" he obsessed as he slammed his palms against the mirror.

Perplexed, he finally gave up and moved back into Glen's sterile halls. And that was when he saw her, Ghost, about forty feet in front of him and moving quickly toward the end of the hall.

Why wasn't she in class?

On impulse, he followed her. Of course, he had no idea what he would say once he caught up with her, but the words would come...like they had at break, sort of.

She was moving fast now, her shoes echoing on the tile floors. He wanted to yell her name, to tell her to wait up, but that would seem too desperate. Despite the fact that he was practically stalking her, he wanted this whole hallway encounter to look like a happy coincidence.

Thatcher was nearly within range when Kaeya disappeared around a corner. And that was when he heard it. A short and piercing yell that echoed like a siren down the empty halls.

Startled, he stopped in his tracks, and that was when he heard it a second time and then a third. It was strange. Almost inhuman.

"Kaeya?" he called as he moved toward the sound. But before he could round the corner, someone grabbed his shoulders from behind.

"Dude, we have to talk," said an out-of-breath voice. It was Max, and he was sweating like he'd run a marathon.

"Not now," answered Thatcher as he pushed Max aside and continued his chase down the hall.

"Thatch, wait!" Max persisted. "It's about your picture. You really need to hear this."

But Thatcher, who had already turned the corner, wasn't listening. He was too busy wondering why the corridor was empty.

The Ghost was gone.

KAEYA

Kaeya heard a knock on her bedroom door, then another. Sleepily, she dropped her heavy hand on the nightstand and began rummaging for her phone to check the time— 7:36 p.m. She'd been asleep for three hours.

"Time for dinner," her father whispered through the door, even though he'd already woken her up.

Dropping her phone back on the nightstand, she rolled over and shut her eyes again. The day had been exhausting. Too exhausting. Sometimes she wondered whether it was even worth it all. This pretending. This battling with a disability that screamed to be noticed, literally.

After a few more unanswered knocks, her father stepped into the room. "How are things going?" he said as he sat on the edge of her bed.

Kaeya sat up and rubbed her eyes while her father waited for an answer.

"I'm not really sure," she said.

THATCHER

The family room was dark and painted in TV-screen blue. His mom, who had completely skipped dinner, was now sitting on the green and beat-up sofa watching some ancient-looking game show rerun. Her eyes were vacant, while the phone rested on her lap...waiting for Dad to call.

Did *love* do this to his mom? Smash into her like a freight train and abandon her on the side of the tracks?

Or was Dad's "love" something else, an antonym of the real thing?

He trudged upstairs toward his bedroom with his own love life to worry about. A love life that revolved around someone who was most likely not longing for his kiss at the moment.

Thatcher flipped on his lamp, trying to ignore the fact that his room was a disaster, an exact replica of the way it had been yesterday and the week before. Pushing aside papers, pens, and textbooks, he kicked off his shoes, plopped onto his bed, and turned on his laptop.

Feeling completely immature, he Googled eight simple words. *How to tell if a girl likes you.* It was dumb, but he had to know. Were there any signs of "like" in the conversation he'd had with her that morning?

He settled on a site called *Wiki-Crush* and began taking the "Is She into U?" quiz that was at the top of the page next to these tiny anime-looking characters with hearts shooting out of their heads. A tiny cat-looking emoji gave him the first question.

Does she punch you, tap you on the head, or lightly bump into you?

"Um, not really," he whispered out loud as he visualized his and Kaeya's morning conversation.

Do her feet point in your direction when she's talking to you?

"What?" he said out loud as he remembered her ankle bracelet and tried to visualize which way her toes were pointing. He had no idea.

Does she smile at you when you're talking?

"Yeah. But Kaeya's always smiling. At everyone."

Thatcher loved her smile, the way she smiled with her whole face as if a smile was who she was. The quiz went on and on, with each question even more ridiculous and generic than the next, and soon Thatcher realized that the website was no fortune-teller. He was sixteen. He'd have to figure out the whole Kaeya thing on his own.

KAEYA

She was still too groggy to go downstairs, so she pulled up the covers, grabbed her phone, and started flipping through the pictures people had posted on her wall. Selfies, coffee cups, a post about cookies, most from people she'd just met at Glen.

But then she saw something that really caught her attention. Thatcher's meme, the same meme Quentin had showed her that morning. One of her friends must have liked it or something, and now it was staring down from the top of the page with the words *Marry Me Martha* in huge yellow letters.

"I am most seriously displeased, Mr. Quentin," she muttered, in words borrowed from *Pride and Prejudice*. And then she scrolled down and saw it, a terrible number, a number that made her cringe—1,821 views. The picture was starting to go viral.

THATCHER

Giving up on the quiz altogether, he decided to check his wall. Lots of likes on his Halo comment. A rant from Jeremy. A couple of videos, a bunch of posts by girls he knew but who already had boyfriends, and then something else, something that made Thatcher flip off his bed and scream so loud that Scout started pounding on his wall to get him to shut up.

His Martha Baines T-shirt! His insane hair and puffy red eyes! It was all there, online and out there for the entire world to see! Someone had posted his school picture!

"No, no, no, no," he mumbled as he saw the number of likes, over a thousand.

He refreshed the page and stared back down at the screen in the hopes that it was some other kid who, by some freak coincidence, had also shown up to school on picture day looking like a total idiot. But it wasn't. The picture staring back at Thatcher Kelly...*was* Thatcher Kelly. He looked like a hopeless loner, and the words *My hamster and only chess partner died, SO MARRY ME MARTHA!* only punctuated the point.

If it had been another picture of him on another day, he might have laughed. But his life had imploded that morning. And they'd taken a picture. And now people were laughing at him as he struggled to crawl out from the wreckage.

Thatcher got up and paced the room like a caged lion, raging at the person who'd cruelly resurrected his school picture from the trash can.

This is not happening, he thought as he picked up the phone. He needed to call someone. Anyone. He decided on Max.

"You saw it, right?" he blurted the second Max picked up the phone.

"Dude, look. I didn't mean to 'like' it," answered his guilty-sounding friend on the other end. "That's what I was trying to tell you today...in the hall."

"You *liked* it?"

"I...I didn't even know it was you at first! Honest!"

"You're supposed to be my friend!" Thatcher was having trouble catching his breath now as he picked up the laptop again.

"Sorry, Thatcher. I'll find out who's posting those and...and then..."

"Those? You mean there's more than one?" interrupted Thatcher, his voice rising to scream-level volume.

"There are, like, twenty of them, Thatch. I tried to tell you at school today but..."

"But you decided to *like* it instead. Thanks a lot, dude. Thanks a lot."

As streams of "sorry" poured from the phone, Thatcher hung up.

He tossed the laptop onto his nightstand as if it were infected and grabbed his keys. He needed to drive. Somewhere. Anywhere. To escape the pain.

4

WEDNESDAY

KAEYA

She realized that Thatcher was a *something*, more than just a blip on her social radar, on Wednesday. Day three. The day she saw him in the hall.

A group of freshman girls were staring as he waited outside language arts. One of them was taking a picture of him on her cell phone. Did he notice?

Yeah, definitely. Kaeya could see it in his eyes as he pretended to ignore them by fiddling with his own phone.

"Hey." She smiled as she walked up from behind and tapped him on top of the head. Startled, he dropped his cell phone on the hard tile floor, which caused the case to fly off.

"I'm *so* sorry!" she gasped as she fell to the floor to help him pick up the pieces.

"N-no worries," he said as he snapped the case back in place. "It does that all the time."

"Yeah, mine too."

For a few minutes neither of them spoke. But Kaeya stayed, blocking the girls' view and standing with Thatcher in a sort of silent solidarity.

"Hey, I think I figured it out," he eventually blurted while looking down at her feet.

"Figured what out?"

"Why you were walking with Hemingway." He smiled, letting her know he was joking.

"Are you still stuck on that stupid dream?" She laughed as she touched him softly on the shoulder. Thatcher's comment was off the wall, but it wasn't *that* off the wall. It was the only connection he had with her, and Kaeya understood.

"Hey, dreams are mirror images of the selves we can't see," he joked in the spacey voice of a psychic. He had a sense of humor. She liked that.

"Okay, Mr. Dream Master. So why did I take a walk with Hemingway?"

Thatcher held his fingers to his temples like a fortune-teller. "Let's see. Hemingway was a modernist writer. And you were walking down a long road, which means you're on some kind of journey," he began. "I know...you're on an existential quest to reinvent yourself in a world gone mad."

"Look at me," she joked. "I'm getting goose bumps."

Thatcher laughed like a little kid, which was definitely endearing.

She was about to tell him about another weird dream she'd had, one about waffles, when her Tourette's interrupted, grabbing her head in a violent twitch and flipping it back against the tile wall.

It hurt. Bad. But she tried to laugh it off like it was an accident.

But Thatcher wasn't buying it. "Ouch," he said softly. He was staring at her now instead of looking down. And that was when she noticed. For the first time. His eyes. They were beautiful.

THATCHER

Thatcher lay on the late-night floor of his book-scattered room and thought of how perfectly the lines aligned with his life. *It was the best of times. It was the worst of times.* Charles Dickens. His favorite author.

The last time he'd checked, his picture, the first variation, had topped five thousand views. And that wasn't all. The memes themselves were multiplying like ridiculous rabbits. His picture was all over the place now, accompanied by stupid, junior-high-level captions like—*My light saber ran out of batteries, so marry me Martha* and *My retainer's stuck to my uvula, so marry me Martha!*—all of them with thousands of views.

But then there was Kaeya, Kaeya with the sky-blue eyes, whose every word came from a deep pool of nice. They'd talked that morning, for the third time in a week...and her feet pointed at him when she did.

Yeah, life was leaning precariously close to an abyss of Dickensian despair. But thinking of her tilted him away from the edge, away and toward the sun.

KAEYA

Someone had posted a video under one of the memes. Kaeya clicked play. It was some sort of concert. Martha Baines, the singer whose T-shirt Thatcher was wearing in the school picture.

"This song's for a little friend of mine," the singer said. "Looks like he's been going through a bit of a rough patch."

The arena audience erupted into laughter as *Marry Me Martha* appeared on the screen behind the stage.

"Now, honey," she told the picture, "it looks like you could use a little lovin'!"

The crowd roared as the opening chords of a song began to play, one that Kaeya already hated. She shut off her phone in disgust. Martha Baines was huge. The clip was huge. Over seven-hundred-thousand-views huge.

"I am *so* not watching the Country Music Awards this year," she told herself as she got back to her homework.

THATCHER

It was past eleven, and he was craving cookies, so he headed downstairs. But something stopped him halfway down the hall. Scout's light. Why was it still on?

He stepped into her pink and princessy palace to see what was up.

Surprisingly, she was wide awake, sitting cross-legged on her Sleeping Beauty bedspread. Since her back was to the door, Thatcher couldn't see her face, but he could tell by the rise and fall of her shoulders that she was crying. Quietly.

"Hey," he said softly, not wanting to startle her. "What's up?"

Scout turned as Thatcher sat on the end of her bed. He waited in silence as she hugged Dash, her oversized stuffed monkey, and wiped tears off with his fur.

"He was gonna take us to Disney World for my birthday," she blurted as another wave of tears hit. She looked fragile and small, a mini version of Mom.

So this is the way a six-year-old handles abandonment, Thatcher thought, *by missing Mickey Mouse instead of Dad.*

Of course, Thatcher didn't tell her that Disney World would have never happened, even if Dad were around. His father was like this Santa Claus imposter, always promising things like trips, Xbox systems, and new cars for Mom. But his presents were hollow boxes wrapped in meaningless words.

"Disney World isn't all that great. It's pretty much the same as Disneyland, and you don't have to take a plane to get there."

"No!" she yelled. "It's better than Disneyland, way, way, better."

Scout hopped off her bed and stomped around the room while she listed everything she'd been told. Disney World was bigger. And there was a monorail. And an Animal Kingdom with live monkeys.

"Don't worry. There are other ways to get to Disney World," Thatcher said as he pulled back her comforter and motioned for her to hop back into bed.

"Other than the monorail?"

"No, other than Dad."

With that, he got up, turned off the light, and headed downstairs.

Once in the hall, he reminded himself Scout was only five, way too young to understand what it had taken him more than a decade to figure out. That the name *Dad* didn't automatically make someone a hero.

5

THURSDAY

KAEYA

Kieran's voice flew across the parking lot as she stepped out of her car.

"Kaeya!" he called from the tennis court gate.

Kaeya played with the bracelets on her wrist, breathing quickly as Kieran weaved his way through row after row of parked cars to get to her, his soccer cleats clicking on the pavement.

What was he doing in the parking lot? He had zero-period soccer. Had he been waiting for her?

A discreet glance in her car's side mirror calmed her racing heart a little. Hair good. Makeup fine.

"Hey," she called as she stood tall and straightened her skirt.

"I saw you pull up," he said with a warm grin on his face. "So...good morning."

There were three circles of sweat on the front of his Glen Canyon T-shirt, and his hair was messed up like he'd been in a wind tunnel, but he looked perfect. As always.

"Well, good morning back," she answered.

Her TS was behaving. So far. She could survive this.

"So what did you think of the homework last night?" he asked as he crossed his arms and leaned against the side of her car.

Math homework? There was math homework?

"Oh, way too hard," she joked, finally remembering that there'd been none.

Kieran laughed, politely, then kicked the ground with the toe of his right cleat. He suddenly looked nervous, and she wondered why.

"Hey, I saw you talking with the *Marry Me* guy yesterday," he finally said. "Are you guys, like, friends?"

It took a second for Kaeya to realize what Kieran was talking about. The *Marry Me* guy...Thatcher. The question surprised her. Why did he want to know?

"Not really. I've talked to him a couple of times. Why?"

Kieran broke eye contact, like he was embarrassed.

"You know about the meme, right?" he asked.

"Well, yeah, I've seen it a couple of times." She didn't want to say too much or seem too enthusiastic in any way. The meme was cruel, and she wondered why Kieran was bringing it up.

"Um, well, they're doing something...at the pep rally today. You might want to let him know."

"Doing something?"

"Yeah, the guys on the team made this PowerPoint, you know, like the ones they always show at the rallies. They're using the *Marry Me Martha* guy.

It's just a joke."

"What kind of a joke?" she answered, her eyes squinting.

"You know, like the whole *My Little Pony* thing when we played Elsinore," he mumbled, apparently taken aback by her sudden change in tone.

Kaeya did know. She'd seen the way they mocked the Stallions by hanging posters of the rivals riding My Little Ponies all over campus. She'd laughed because it was funny. But this wasn't the same thing. This time they'd be using Thatcher, a real person.

"Well, that's not cool," she finally said as she dipped back into her car to grab her phone. They were strong words, but she needed to say them, to be true to herself.

Kieran nodded, his hands in his pockets, head down. And a sudden feeling fell on Kaeya like a heavy fog—disappointment. Did Kieran have something to do with the meme?

Never. The meme couldn't be his fault. He was trying to warn Thatcher...through her. That was good. Wasn't it? She searched his eyes for signs of innocence. She couldn't tell.

"Kieran," she called as she picked her book bag off the roof of her car and got ready to leave.

He looked up.

"His name's not the Marry Me Guy. It's Thatcher." Her tone sounded harsh, too harsh. Why was she defending Thatcher? She barely knew the guy.

Kieran nodded. "Right...Thatcher," he said, biting his top lip. He was adorable. Too adorable to be cruel.

They stood in silence for a few more seconds until the bell rang. "So I'll see you in math?" he said.

"Sure," she said with a small wave.

"Way to scare a guy away, Kaeya," she muttered as she watched him jog away.

THATCHER

Thatcher approached the gym with heavy steps. As usual, the decibels were off the chart, with screaming kids and a marching band that was never made to play indoors causing auditory chaos.

A gorilla with a Glen Canyon T-shirt reached up for a high five. Reluctantly, Thatcher obliged, giving the furry paw a halfhearted slap.

He actually liked sports. But the rallies were ridiculous, and an entire school day rearranged so that the school's rock-star athletes could be praised made absolutely no sense.

Climbing to the highest point of the bleachers, he leaned back against one of a zillion peppy butcher-paper posters that lined the walls, and waited for the spectacle to begin.

Of course, the pep rally was for the soccer team. Soccer was *huge* at Glen, just as huge as football. The school had been CIF state champions three years running, and the current team was heading into the second half of the season undefeated. Three Glen alumni had even competed in the Olympics, their life-sized pictures lording over the gym lobby like medieval kings.

When the entire student body had finished cramming into the bleachers, the room went dark. It was time. The spotlights began a dizzying dance as the band launched into an awful cover of *Eye of the Tiger*. Then there was smoke as gladiator-like figures emerged from the back of the gym, the soccer team.

Students cheered like trained monkeys as the team streamed down a center aisle toward a stage set up on one end of the basketball court. They were all wearing suits and ties, a tradition on game days, and pumping their arms in the air in rhythm with the music.

When the team finally settled onto the stage and the music died down, the team captain, an overly extroverted senior with the arms of a weight lifter, took the microphone. "So whom of you out there wants to win first place?" he screamed into the mike.

It's who. Who of you wants to win the title? Thatcher edited in his head.

"And whom of you is going to be out there tomorrow night to support us?"

The students, who couldn't care less about grammar, roared their approval, then continued to roar as another player took the mike, Quentin, the team's goalkeeper.

"Listen, guys!" he bellowed while trying to suppress a laugh. "We put together a little scouting report of our opponents, Seal Beach."

The crowd laughed because they knew what was coming next. Something funny. Like always.

The lights dimmed again. More music, the *Charlie Brown* theme song, as a giant white screen rolled down from the ceiling.

Thatcher froze as the screen came into focus.

The image. It was him. In all his picture-day glory. "Scouting Report" read the title.

Another slide appeared. This time, someone had Photoshopped an opposing player's head onto Thatcher's body. *I've given up more goals than any other goalie this season. SO MARRY ME MARTHA!* read the words beneath.

As soon as that slide faded, another took its place, one that showed another Thatcher / Seal Beach mutation. Quentin read the first line. "I've only scored four goals all season," and everyone in the gym screamed the rest.

"SO MARRY ME MARTHA!"

The slides kept coming, one after another.

I've lost seventy-eight percent of my games.

I have a goal differential of negative twenty-one.

I'm scared of Glen!

And with each picture, the gym would erupt into peals of laughter while chanting "SO MARRY ME MARTHA!"

Thatcher felt like fleeing the gym like a criminal, but instead he sat quietly. Until the PowerPoint ran its course and the lights turned back on, until the principal gave a speech and the pep rally came to a close...until he had had enough.

KAEYA

Kaeya hardly ever got angry, about anything. But she was furious now. At the soccer team for creating the PowerPoint. At the administration for being completely oblivious to what was going down on their own campus. At the hundreds of students who laughed callously with each slide.

To them, Thatcher was just another Internet character—like Grumpy Cat or Star Wars Kid—a character who dwelled in some online dimension where feelings didn't exist and pain wasn't real. Kaeya winced at the thought of Thatcher being in the gym.

And then there was Kieran. She watched as he stepped off the stage. Did he feel anything? Anything at all?

Had she not looked up to check the scoreboard clock, she would have missed it, Thatcher bolting down the stairs on the opposite side of the gym. His steps were deliberate, and he had a strange expression on his face, one that she couldn't read.

A voice popped into her head. *Talk to him. Tell him that the entire student body is insane and that he is a far nobler human than the lot of them.*

"Thatcher!" she called as she reached the floor where hundreds of bodies converged in a mass exodus.

It was obvious he couldn't hear, so she began pushing her way across the crowded gym floor in an attempt to cut him off at the door.

"Thatcher!" Kaeya called again. He was near the exit now, impossibly far away. She watched as he disappeared under the scoreboard and out the door.

When Kaeya finally made it outside, Thatcher was nowhere to be seen.

Shielding her eyes from the afternoon sun, she caught a glimpse of someone standing in the distance. He was kneeling next to a table, head down, feverishly writing something on one of those ancient, school-issued iPads. Was it him?

She paced the quad's perimeter to get a closer look. It was.

"Hey," she called as she approached from behind. But Thatcher, who was now climbing up on a lunch table, seemed oblivious.

Stunned, Kaeya watched as he raised the iPad over his head like some human billboard. He must have written something, but his back was toward her, so she couldn't see.

Initially, no one noticed, but within a minute or so a crowd of onlookers began to gather, walking up to the lunch table to get a better look.

Curious, she inched her way forward, but before reaching reading range, the quad erupted into a verbal war zone. A senior stood on a planter and yelled something while students cheered. A girl she recognized from student leadership threw an empty water bottle. A couple of red-faced soccer players screamed profanities.

What did the guy write?

THATCHER

Had he been given a do-over, he would have written something clever, maybe a Shakespearean insult like WOULD THOU WERT CLEAN ENOUGH TO SPIT UPON! Then no one in the crowd would have understood, and the nightmare that was to come could have been avoided. But in a total rage, all he'd been able to think of was

Glen Canyon Soccer sucks!

Quentin Elliot sucks!

You all suck!

It was junior high-ish and dumb, but Thatcher was seeing red now, and he didn't care.

As the scribbled insults flew across the screen, a couple of students jokingly clapped, while others, seemingly upset, screamed insults of their own.

Good. He wanted them to yell, to lose control, to snap like he had. Because he wanted them all to feel like he did, hopeless and out of control.

KAEYA

Without warning, the scene blew up, like a land mine in some tragic war movie, a movie she didn't want to see.First, Quentin, who was at least six foot two, stepped up to Thatcher with this *You're going to do what I tell you to do* look on his face. He said something, but Thatcher didn't answer. Then Quentin clawed for the iPad, but Thatcher jerked it away. There were more words from Quentin, followed by a defiant silence as

Thatcher held the iPad even higher.

Thatcher finally stepped off the table and put his iPad in his book bag. Kaeya breathed a sigh of relief. The confrontation was over, or so she thought.

But as Thatcher started walking away, Quentin said something. At first, Thatcher didn't react. He just stood there on the sidewalk. But after a few seconds, he suddenly turned and barreled into Quentin head first.

There was no time for Quentin to push back or scream or do anything. He fell like a dying redwood. There was a dull thud as the back of his head hit the edge of a planter, and there was blood, more blood than Kaeya had ever seen.

Kaeya watched in slow motion. As people screamed. As Thatcher stepped backward, covering his mouth with both hands. As Quentin lay motionless on the cement.

And she wondered, was he dead?

Thatcher

The entire afternoon was one of sirens, screams, and questions, and he wanted more than anything to go home.

It was almost four, and his mom and dad had been in Mr. Blakely's office for nearly an hour, along with a scary-looking lady from the school district. Mom hadn't acknowledged Thatcher on her way in. She was ashamed, and he was too.

Thatcher leaned over in his chair in the empty waiting room, head resting firmly in his palms. *Stupid, stupid, stupid,* he thought as the images looped in his head. The sound of skull on cement. The blood pooling underneath Quentin's head. The paramedics rolling Quentin's motionless body away. Teachers and counselors were sent out to comfort crying students. But not him. He was the enemy now. He'd seen it in their eyes.

When Principal Blakely escorted him into the front office, he'd nearly passed out. Two police officers waiting for him in the lobby. With horrifying visions of juvenile detention swirling around in his head, he'd told them the truth. About the iPad message. About Quentin's threat to "make him" take it down, about the tug of war with the tablet and his sudden loss of control.

But he never mentioned the meme. No way. Telling them about *Marry Me Martha* would've led to school-wide assemblies on bullying, and hand-painted ASB posters about Internet civility. He'd had enough humiliation already. Thank you.

Luckily, the officers left long before Mom arrived. She wouldn't have been able to handle that. "It was just a schoolyard fight," one officer had told the principal, much to Thatcher's relief.

Except for the gray-haired receptionist who eyed him like a convict every time she walked past on her way to the copy machine, he was totally alone. As the clock ticked. As a janitor's vacuum echoed from a distant classroom. As Judgment Day approached.

KAEYA

Crying was okay when she was reading a book or watching a sappy Hallmark movie, but not now, not in public. Tears would make her Tourette's rage, and she needed to hold it together, at least until she pulled out of the school parking lot.

When she reached the front steps, she quickened her pace. All she wanted to do now was go home and escape into a book or a TV show or a bowl of ice cream, anything to forget the image of Quentin's head hitting brick.

But the minute she reached the parking lot, she knew. The ice cream would have to wait. Someone was leaning against the dent in her driver's side door. Kieran.

"You okay?" he asked.

"Not really," she said as she fumbled with her keys. "Awful day"—*cough*—"I just want to go home and take a nap."

"No kidding," he said, his blond hair blowing in the breeze that flowed in warm waves across the asphalt. He was staring at her, gently, as if her pain was his.

"Kaeya, if it helps you sleep any better, I'm sorry."

"Sorry? For what?" she asked as she turned to cough away another tic.

"For the whole *Marry Me Martha* thing. I mean, it was only a joke, but I probably should have said something when they were planning for the rally."

His comments were proof. His heart matched his looks. He cared.

"Hey, this wasn't your fault," she said, biting her lip to keep a new round of tears from beginning their march. Kieran nodded. He looked sad.

"So how is he?" she asked.

"I don't know. They took him to Corona Regional. I'm heading over there right now." Kieran stuck his hands in the pockets of his jeans. "Um, wanna come with?"

Did she want to come? With Kieran? Yes, absolutely yes. But *wanting* to and *being able* to were two entirely different questions. In her present stressed-out state, he'd notice her Tourette's for sure. And she wasn't ready for that, not yet, not today.

Kaeya stared at her feet, waiting for some magical explanation to pop into her head and save the day. But the magic never came. "I really want to...for Quentin. But I can't," she finally blurted.

"Oh, okay, I get it," Kieran said as he broke eye contact for the first time in the conversation.

She wanted to grab his wide shoulders with both hands and scream, *No, you don't get it! Not at all! I would love to drive to the hospital with you. I would love to drive anywhere with you!* But instead, she smiled hollowly as Kieran gave her a quick hug and walked dejectedly away.

Then she waited until he walked across the parking lot, got in his car, and drove away. And when she couldn't see his car anymore, she got in her car and cried, for Quentin, for Thatcher, and for Kieran...who had probably just given her his last hug.

THATCHER

The brick-walled office felt claustrophobic as Thatcher crossed the threshold. The stern-looking woman from the district was there, along with his parents and Mr. Blakely, who motioned for him to sit.

"Son, do you realize what a serious matter this is?" said Mr. Blakely, his breathing labored.

Thatcher nodded as everyone in the room stared.

"You've sent a student to the hospital, Thatcher...to the hospital," the principal began. "Fortunately for you, Quentin's family have decided to let the district handle this incident. So, as for the police, they are no longer involved."

No surprise there. So far so good.

"But as you may or may not know, Corona Unified does have a no-tolerance policy, and there will be consequences for your actions."

Consequences. No surprise either. Thatcher thought two, maybe three, Saturday detentions? Jacob Hadley had a single day of Saturday hours for decking Anders Larson during PE. He could handle that.

District Lady was talking now, looking up from her notes, her beady brown eyes bearing down on Thatcher like a guard dog.

"You'll be serving a fifteen-day suspension," she said.

Suspension? Fifteen days? Now he was surprised. Shocked actually. The suspension would go on his record, limiting his university options. He'd fall behind on his schoolwork, limiting his options even more. And Kaeya, he'd completely lose touch with her.

"But...but it was an accident," he reasoned in the calmest voice he could muster.

Mom shot him a look, one that said *shut up*, while Dad tapped his foot like he was playing kick drum in a speed-metal band.

"Oh, so you *accidentally* tripped on a banana peel and bumped into him?" said District Lady. The vein on her left temple bulged as she waited for an answer, but Thatcher, who hated sarcasm, said nothing.

"You and I both know...it wasn't an accident," she finally answered for him.

He wanted to scream, *And my school picture being publically mocked at a school-sponsored assembly wasn't an accident either*, but Shakespeare held him back.

Give thy thoughts no tongue! screamed the playwright from the well-worn *Hamlet* file in Thatcher's brain.

"I know. I know," Thatcher responded out loud,which annoyed District Lady, who had no idea he was talking to the Bard of Avon, not her.

"Watch your tone, young man," she said with a stern look of warning in her eyes.

Arguing was out of the question, so Thatcher took a deep breath, lowered his voice, and tried reasoning with them.

"Mr. Blakely, I know...I know I blew it today, but I've never done anything even remotely violent before. Can't you just give me another chance? Please?"

His tone was beginning to grow desperate, too desperate, causing District Lady to lean away from him as if he were going to overturn the table or something, which, except for flipping a Monopoly board over when he was eight, was something he'd never in his life considered doing.

He looked toward his parents. "Mom. Dad. Say something."

Mom crossed her arms, a neutral nation in a room full of enemies, while Dad opened his mouth to say something, then quickly closed it again.

"The suspension will be in-house," said Mr. Blakely, entirely ignoring Thatcher's pleas. "You're to report to Mrs. DeGeau's room first thing tomorrow morning. Her room is out back where the automotive science building once was."

Mr. Blakely went on to explain the rules of captivity. His teachers would give him independent-study work. He would arrive at school early so as not to mix with the other students. He would sign out with Mrs. DeGeau at the end of each day.

"And one more thing," District Lady interrupted. "Before returning to the normal school population, you'll be required to complete a character education project."

"What kind of project?" he asked.

"Mrs. DeGeau will give you the details when you check in on Monday," she answered coldly.

The rest of the meeting flew by in a hazy blur.

The signing of the suspension papers. The somber shaking of the hands. His mother's teary-eyed flight from the office.

With Mr. Blakely back in his office and District Lady well on her way out the front door, everyone was gone except for Dad.

He wanted to say something. Thatcher could tell. But his words were rusty and stuck, like an old gate, and neither he nor Thatcher had the strength to pry it loose. So instead of saying "I'm sorry," or "It's not so bad," or even the cursory "We're disappointed in you," Dad patted Thatcher's shoulder, as if he were a dog, not a son, then walked away...with millions of unspoken words buried deep in the pockets of his cheap suit.

6

FRIDAY

KAEYA

Kaeya was swimming with dolphins when the alarm on her phone shouted WAKE UP! in annoying foghorn-like tones. It was early, way too early, for this. She loved sleep, adored it like Christmas, and in her opinion, mornings should have been outlawed.

Sitting up in bed, she groggily waited for the tics to show. Like a morning weatherman, she could usually predict how bad the day's storm would be before it began. She stretched out her arms and stared at her hands. Nothing. No shakes, no grunting, no yelled *HAs* into the air. A good sign.

She willed herself out of bed and turned towardthe mirror. "Kiss me, Kieran. I'm yours," she joked as she stared down her poofy-eyed, messy-haired image.

As always, she gave mirror self a high five before heading to the bathroom. It was a fresh, new day, and if she looked hard enough, she'd find it, hope, stretching its arms out to meet her.

At least that was what her mom used to say.

THATCHER

Mom's lips were moving, but he couldn't hear. The EDM music pulsing through his headphones was way too loud for conversation. He set his backpack down and turned the music off.

"Don't be mad. Okay?" she repeated as she kissed the top of his head.

"I'm not mad," he mumbled as he brushed past.

The antisocial tone of his voice surprised him, and he suddenly realized how stressed he was. The fact that he was running late for his in-house suspension only compounded the problem.

As Thatcher moved toward the door, his mother remained motionless, her head down like a defeated boxer. Feeling guilty, he turned back and gave her a hug. She hugged him back, tightly, like he was five years old again. Soon, Thatcher felt another pair of arms hugging the side of his legs, Scout's.

He was for sure going to be late now, but he didn't want to leave.

"Wanna talk about it?" said his mom as she released her grip and wiped a few tears from her eyes.

He did want to talk about it. The crushing guilt he had about sending Quentin to the hospital. The humiliating meme. The stupid suspension. But not now, not to her. She couldn't even figure out her own life at the moment, and he didn't want to pile on to her list of worries.

"It'll be okay," he assured her as he headed out the door.

But he wasn't sure if things *would* work themselves out. In fact, he was pretty sure that they wouldn't. Because life was too heavy at the moment, too heavy for his sixteen-year-old arms to carry.

KAEYA

Even though it was October in California, it felt like a London winter. Fitting weather, Kaeya thought as she made her way past the administration building. Cold. Like the mood at Glen.

Everywhere Kaeya looked, people were talking about the accident, speculating whether Quentin was okay, gossiping about how the *Marry Me Martha* guy went psycho.

Kaeya only caught one smile that morning, Kieran's. He laughed as he plowed into her in front of the attendance office.

"Whoa!" he gasped as he grabbed her forearms to keep her from falling.

"Oh my gosh," she said, her heart racing. "You almost made me Quentin's roommate."

Kaeya instantly realized how insanely insensitive that must have sounded. "Okay, that totally came out wrong," she said. "It's just that I almost fell, and Quentin's in the hospital...and I'm *so* not making this any better!"

"No, you're not." He laughed again, exposing rows of perfectly white teeth.

Cool. He had a sense of humor. And...she didn't think his running into her was a coincidence. Even more cool.

"So how is he?" she asked softly, biting her lower lip in anticipation of bad news.

"He cracked his skull and has a concussion, but he's stable. At least that's what he told me yesterday. They're keeping him in the hospital for a while, to run some more tests."

"So he's talking. That's good. Right?"

"Yeah, that's good," Kieran answered gently. "Looks like he's been run over by a train though."

"He couldn't have looked any worse than he did on Friday. I still can't get the image out of my head."

Kieran nodded, stared at something on the ground for a while, then looked up. "I would have called you with an update...but I didn't have your number."

Kaeya's heart skipped. Was this his way of asking for it?

"Well, you should have it then," she said.

"Cool," he said as he pulled out his phone. "That way I can..."

"Give me updates?" she finished. She was smiling. And so was he.

"Yeah...and other information," he said.

Was he was flirting? Actually flirting? With her? Amazing!

"Okay, I'm ready when you are," he said. "Fire away."

Kieran listened intently as she rattled off the numbers, and when he was done punching them into his contact list, he leaned in and gave her a hug.

"I'll text you," he said with a smile.

"Definitely," she answered softly as she watched him walk away.

Kieran's confidence amazed her, the way he knew who he was and what he wanted, without being stuck up. Her heart was spinning toward the point of no return...and that terrified her.

THATCHER

With a photocopied map in hand, Thatcher trekked toward the back part of campus where his "prison" was supposed to be. He'd heard of this wooded part of campus, the area that some students called Area 51, but he'd never actually been there.

The closer he got to the highlighted circle on the map, the more isolated he felt. The sidewalk was cracked and crumbling, and there were weeds everywhere. To make matters worse, there were no classrooms to be seen, at least not in the normal sense. The only building he could see was an ominously old, warehouse-looking structure that looked dilapidated beyond recognition.

This must be it, he thought as he awkwardly searched for a door or any opening through which to enter. But he was out of luck. The only entryway seemed to be a massive garage-looking door, but that appeared to be rusted shut. Was he in the wrong place?

Thatcher looked back at the map, then up again before venturing down a little stone path that twisted and turned toward the east side of the rusty warehouse. The weeds were higher here, with some reaching over his head, but soon he spied it, a single door painted sky blue and adorned with hand-painted sunflowers. The whimsical door seemed out of place on the corrugated metal wall, but it added warmth to the dystopian-like scene.

A first set of knocks yielded no results. So he tried knocking again. This time louder.

Still no answer.

Next, he tried the handle. The door was unlocked. He pulled it open slowly. The lights were on, and there was music. Was he supposed to just walk in?

Cautiously, he inched his way through the threshold and began taking inventory of his jail cell for the next few weeks.

Instantly, he could tell. This wasn't a prison. The room was huge, with purple and red walls and a tall vaulted ceiling. The entire scene screamed artsy coffeehouse, not classroom. In fact, the place even smelled like coffee.

A circle of plush chairs sat in the center of the polished concrete floors, next to the hulk of a graffiti-painted Cadillac. And there was art *everywhere*. Framed posters of famous writers lined the only brick wall in the place, and a gigantic antique mirror was perched between two rows of aesthetically organized auto-shop junk.

"No way," he whispered aloud as he scanned his surroundings.

"Thatcher Kelly I presume?" a female voice announced, nearly causing Thatcher to swallow his gum. It came from a cluttered desk in a far corner, the only visible remnant of the auto-shop classroom that once was.

The voice belonged to a woman wearing hip librarian-looking glasses. She was surprisingly young and had Chinese symbols tattooed on both of her wrists. This, along with the vintage dress she was wearing, made her look more singer-songwriter than teacher.

"Sorry. I...I knocked, but no one answered," he blurted, "so I just sort of came in."

"'Fear not,'" she said as she stood up and walked toward him. "'Forcing oneself into the unknown is the occupation of the bold.'" She motioned toward the quote-plastered wall behind her. "Sir Devon Paxton, 1854."

The quote was Sir *David* Paxton's, not Devon, but Thatcher knew enough about making a good first impression to keep his mouth shut. So instead, he nodded politely and waited for the woman, who he assumed was Mrs. DeGeau, to explain how this whole in-house suspension thing was supposed to work.

But she never did. Apparently in no rush to recite rules, she simply walked back to her disaster of a desk, where she proceeded to shuffle papers around while humming along to the French pop song now blaring through the speakers.

After a minute or so, she looked up. "There's a coffeemaker in the back, one of those fancy Keurig kinds. It's easy to use."

Thatcher looked toward the back of the room. Yup, there was a coffeemaker there, two of them actually, along with enough coffee refills to energize an army of sloths. But he wasn't about to fill up. The whole Bohemian vibe of the place was confusing, and he wondered whether there was some hidden catch to the Starbucks-like suspension he'd fallen into.

With nothing else to do, he made his way to the center of the cavernous room and plopped down on pillow-covered velvet sofa. And hands on knees, he waited for five, ten, fifteen minutes until he couldn't handle it anymore.

"So, um, Mr. Blakely said something about a character education project?" he asked.

Mrs. DeGeau stood and smiled, as if she'd been awoken by some magical incantation. She strolled toward the center of the room and took a seat in the purple chair across from him. Leaning forward, she looked sternly into his eyes, as if he were a mystery that needed to be solved.

"So why didn't you tell him?" she began.

"Umm, tell who what?"

"The principal. About *Marry Me Martha*. I was at the pep rally. Why didn't you say anything?"

Thatcher's heart sank. Up until then, he thought his humiliation was isolated to the world of teens. But now he knew otherwise. He looked down and fiddled with his watch. "I don't know. Kind of embarrassing, I guess," he eventually said.

"Look, Thatcher," she continued, "I've been directed to watch you like a hawk. I'm supposed to call campus security when I leave the room. I'm even supposed to have someone escort you when you need to use the restroom, but..."

Her sentences slowed to a stop, as if the words were weighing on her like buckets of cement. "Thatcher. Did you mean to hurt him?" she finally said.

Thatcher stared at the ground for a while before looking up. "Not at all," he said. "I was leaving, and then he said something, and, I don't know, I just snapped. And I was—"

"I thought so," she interrupted as she popped up, straightened her skirt, and walked back to her desk. "Be good while I'm gone," she called as she grabbed a pile of file folders and headed for the door.

"Mrs. DeGeau. Wait!" Thatcher called.

She turned around.

"What about my project?"

"Patience, my friend," she said. "The muse hasn't whispered to me yet."

The muse? DeGeau was bizarre. In fact, the entire gallery was bizarre, surreal, like a Kafka novel...and Thatcher liked Kafka.

KAEYA

Kaeya heard music as she entered the math building. It was loud and played poorly on an acoustic guitar. The culprit was standing next to a bunch of balloons, singing to a red-faced junior that Kaeya recognized, Amber.

Yay! she thought. It was a *Lanterns ask*. Her first one. She'd heard all about them from Neyma—messages dropped from planes, massive question-marked sentences scrawled in chalk, romantic announcements over the PA system.

Even better was the fact that Kieran was there, along with a zillion other students. His arms were crossed as he listened to the dude pour out his off-key heart. She moved next to him. He looked over and grinned. Amazing.

As the way-too-long song continued, Kaeya inwardly cheered as the dude botched his way through. Sure, lines like *You always act so sweet, when you smile, when you walk, when you eat* were totally cliché. But so what? It was totally romantic and sweet, and when the girl practically tackled the guy at the end, Kaeya couldn't help but clap.

"Ed Sheeran, he's definitely not." Kieran laughed.Kaeya punched him on the forearm. "That's mean," she said. "I thought it was sweet."

Kieran cocked his head and stared at her, a weird smile on the edge of his lips.

"What?" she asked.

"Nothing."

"Then stop staring at me," she joked as she punched him again, harder.

Kieran kicked the ground. "I'm not staring at you. Just taking mental notes."

Mental notes? The words intrigued her. Mental notes for what? Kaeya would have stayed out here in the hall, her eyes boring into his soul until she found out. But her tics were on the way. She could feel the nervous adrenaline now, pulsing through her veins like electricity.

She shoved her hands in her pockets and rocked on her heels. *Hold it together, girl. Just a little longer. You can do this.*

Kieran's mouth was moving, snapping her back to the moment.

"So you're the Hallmark-movie type, I take it?"

"Not really. Too dramatic. To tell you the truth, I'd hate being asked to Lanterns like this. Too much attention. I like my romance sweet and simple: violets picked from a garden, a heartfelt sticky note on my windshield. Something like that."

Kieran pointed toward the Lanterns couple. They were taking selfies of themselves holding the balloons. "Did they go all out like this at your old school?"

"Sometimes, for prom mainly."

"Well, this is nothing. Just wait until the week before Lanterns. It gets crazy around here."

"Crazy good or crazy bad?"

"Depends on if the right person asks you to the dance, I guess." He grinned.

Right then, all Kaeya could think of was how perfect his lips were, perfect and sweet and organic. And how if he kissed her right there in the hall, she wouldn't mind. But deep in the middle of the daydream, it came, an unannounced squeal followed by a violent, neck-jerking tic.

"Whoa! Are you okay?" asked Kieran, who wasn't smiling anymore.

Kaeya frantically swiped her shirt. "Stupid *bug*," she lied. "Gross!"

"Here, let me see." He laughed as he reached for her neck and examined it for any signs of life. Kaeya would have let his hands linger for as long as he wanted them to, but she knew that the twitch was the first of many.

"Look. I've got to go," she said as she ducked under his outstretched arms.

"Okay?" he said, sounding guilty. He felt bad for touching her neck. She could tell. And *she* felt bad that *he* felt bad. But there was nothing she could do about it, not now as another tic, a smaller one, grabbed hold of her face.

Without a good-bye, Kaeya bolted for the exit.

"Hey, aren't you going to calc?" Kieran called as she reached the end of the hall.

"I can't," she said as she pushed through the double doors. And this time she was telling the truth.

THATCHER

The morning had been exhaustingly boring, and though he'd fought to stay awake in case Mrs. DeGeau returned, he'd lost the battle.

After about an hour or so, something woke Thatcher up, a scream sort of sound that echoed off the walls. As the sound grew louder, he began to realize that he wasn't at home. He was at school, in the gallery.

He turned sideways on the sofa and tried to fall back asleep. But the squeaking persisted. Then he heard something. Whispering. Someone was there.

"Poke him," someone said. It was a male voice, one he didn't recognize.

"I'm not gonna poke him!" whispered someone else, a girl.

Groggily, he opened his eyes and took inventory of his surroundings. The French music was still playing, Tolstoy was on the floor...and someone was staring at him, a stylish-looking Asian kid with headphones around his neck. He was holding a video camera, and he wasn't alone.

"*Kaeya*!" he blurted as he shot up on the sofa.

"Hey, sleepyhead," she whispered. Her tone was soft and endearing, but it nearly sent Thatcher into a panic attack.

He checked his mouth for signs of drool. He straightened his T-shirt. He ran his hands through his hair. He wasn't ready for this...at all.

The guy was filming now, which freaked Thatcher out. It was *Marry Me Martha* all over again, only this time live.

"Put the camera down!" said Kaeya as she whipped a pillow across his face.

She turned to Thatcher. "Don't worry. He's deleting that." To prove her point, Kaeya grabbed the camera out of his hands and deleted the footage herself.

She put the camera on the coffee table and pushed a cup in his direction. "I made you some coffee," she said.

He noticed her nail polish, blue, the same as her eyes.

He hated coffee, but he reached for it anyway. He would have reached for a cup of dirt had she offered.

"She mixes in Nutella. One sip will make you fall in love," Sam interrupted.

But Thatcher didn't need a cup of coffee to fall in love. Kaeya of the dark hair and baby-blue eyes was sitting inches away from him. The scene was surreal and exhilarating and a nightmare all at once. He had no idea what to do with it.

"So this is where they're locking you up," she commented as he took his first sip. She was smiling, butshe still looked nervous. Thatcher wondered why.

"Yeah, for three weeks," he answered as he watched her fiddle with the rubber bands on her wrists.

"I'm sorry," she said.

"No, it's...it's fine. I mean, there are worse places to spend three weeks."

"Like Mr. Selznick's class?"

"Yeah, *especially* Mr. Selznick's class." Thatcher laughed.

After taking another nervous sip, then another, he set the cup back on the table. "Seriously though, this place is cool. It's like a Starbucks-slash-art museum."

"The art classes used to be in here, before they built the new building," said Sam, who was sitting cross-legged on the sofa and sipping away on his own cup. "Mrs. DeGeau added the sofas and stuff, and it turned into the 'Gallery.' That's what me and Arwen here call it."

Arwen, the fairy princess in *Lord of the Rings*.

Thatcher glanced over at Kaeya's shiny black hair

and immediately understood.

"Have you..." Kaeya froze midsentence, coughed a couple of times, then grabbed her neck as if she was trying to hold her head straight. After a few seconds of silence, she continued. "Have you met Mrs. DeGeau yet?"

"Yeah, this morning," Thatcher answered. "But then she just took off."

"She's always taking off," explained Sam. "She taught art last year, but there weren't enough students this semester. So now they basically use her to do all the boring jobs around campus."

Sam kept talking, but Thatcher wasn't paying attention. He was too focused on Kaeya. She looked extremely uncomfortable, with her mouth kind of freaking out and her neck twitching. He tried not to stare, and was doing a good job of it...until she yelled into the air.

The sharp *HA!* startled him, and he nearly fell off his seat.

Sam, on the other hand, leaned back on the sofa as if nothing had happened, completely oblivious to the fact that the girl sitting next to him had just screamed like an animal.

Before he had a chance to recover, Kaeya squealed again, louder this time, making Thatcher wonder whether he was the subject of a YouTube prank or something.

She looked over at Sam. "Do you mind if I talk to Thatcher alone?" she asked.

Sam picked up his backpack and headed for a desk in the far corner of the building. "No prob," he called over his shoulder. "Gotta a screenplay to work on anyway. Scene ten. 'The Escape.'"

There was another squeal, then an awkward silence. She looked embarrassed—no, worse than embarrassed, mortified—and Thatcher had no idea how to respond.

KAEYA

When Kaeya first heard about Thatcher's arrival from Sam that morning, she'd freaked. The Gallery was her refuge, her hideout, her school-approved tic-releasing paradise. She needed the place to be student-free.

Sure, there was Sam. But he was okay. He'd been in the Gallery since day one and was usually so lost in his screenplay that he hardly noticed. But Thatcher, that was different. He was kind of, well, attractive. And she didn't really know him. And what if he turned out to be a compulsive gossip? The entire campus would find out. Kieran would find out. She needed to deal with this. Now.

"Thatcher," she began slowly, "I need to tell you something."

He leaned forward on the sofa and fiddled with the handle on his Van Gogh mug. She had his attention.

"I have something called Tourette's syndrome," she began. It was the *I Have TS* speech, the speech she'd given on every first day of school since fifth grade, the speech that she'd come to Glen Canyon to escape.

Thatcher seemed nervous, but was trying to act nonchalant. "Um, that's the disease where people scream profanities, right?"

"Well, yeah, some people with Tourette's cuss. Most don't though. I don't. I tic a lot. Tics are these involuntary muscle movements. I also vocalize, which means I make sounds like the squeaks you just heard."

The words felt flat like an old beach ball, but she checked off the boxes anyway. TS was a neurodevelopmental disorder. It was hereditary. One in a hundred people got it. It got worse with stress. And no, it didn't hurt.

Thatcher was concentrating, like he was trying to understand her heart as well as her words. She liked that.

"So basically I make weird faces and weird sounds, sometimes simultaneously. But don't worry. It's not contagious," she teased. But he didn't laugh. Probably afraid to.

"So how long have you had it?" he asked.

"Since the beginning of fourth grade. But when my mom died, the tics got a lot worse. It got to the point where my dad wanted to homeschool me. But I put up a fight."

Thatcher changed the subject. "I'm sorry...about your mom."

"Oh, that was a long time ago." Kaeya didn't want to go there right now. She didn't need another person feeling sorry for her. She changed the subject.

"Anyway, they let me come in here whenever I want. It was part of the deal when I transferred from Centennial."

"So that's why you're always leaving class?"

"Yeah. I needed to a place where I could be

Kaeya Garay for a while, not Kaeya, asterisk, the girl with Tourette's. My old school psychologist was totally against the change. But I begged my dad until I finally wore him out."

"So nobody at Glen knows?"

"That's the plan. My plan."

"The psych here was cool about it though. She set me up with Mrs. DeGeau. Told all my teachers to let me leave whenever I needed a break."

"So how do you keep up with your work?"

Another set of tics interrupted the conversation, and Kaeya waited patiently for them to pass. "I'm basically on independent study now. The teachers give me the work a week in advance, and I usually end up finishing it in here. But I go to class sometimes, when I feel calm enough."

Kaeya was about to tell him to keep it a secret. But she didn't have to.

"Don't worry. I won't tell," he said.

And that was when she knew. She could trust him. With everything.

THATCHER

The house was silent. The lights were off. It was way too late. But Thatcher couldn't sleep. He was remembering: the smell of her perfume, the way her head tilted when she was trying to understand, the sound of her bracelets jingling when she was trying to get a point across.

They'd talked for over an hour, a complete hour, and he could have talked for a thousand more. Because her voice was a balm that made him forget about *Marry Me Martha* with its three hundred thousand views. About Dad who didn't care. About Mom who was presently crying herself to sleep.

He turned on his side and closed his eyes. And for the first time ever, he couldn't wait for school on Monday.

KAEYA

It was way late, but Kaeya couldn't sleep. She'd told Thatcher about her Tourette's, and he didn't run away screaming. In fact, they'd talked for over an hour, and it was okay, totally okay.

Maybe there was hope. For Kieran and her. If Thatcher didn't mind, why would he? She stared up at the ceiling, dreaming of the possibility...until her phone lit up. A text.

She sat up and picked up her phone. "No way. No Way. No *way*!" she said as she looked at the screen. The text was from Kieran.

Hey, it said.

Hey back, she answered, playing it cool, trying not to seem overexcited.

As soon as she hit Send, her phone lit up again.

Quentin gets to go home in a few days.

Kaeya texted back a smiley face.

7

SATURDAY

THATCHER

He'd slept perfectly, so perfectly that he'd nearly forgotten about his nightmarish week. Kaeya had everything to do with that.

He could have remained in this Kaeya-induced state for hours had he not gone online.

The concert footage of Martha Baines mocking him in front of a packed arena was everywhere, which catapulted *Marry Me Martha* past the million-view mark.

The sight sucked the air out of his lungs, leaving a dull ache where there used to be hope. If Kaeya hadn't seen *Marry Me Martha* yet, she definitely would, and then she'd avoid him like the plague.

He'd been stupid to think that there was enough magic in the universe to actually have a chance. The *Marry Me Martha* guy wasn't some made-up character. It was him.

Thatcher took a deep breath. *This will blow over eventually*, he told himself. *Just keep moving.*

KAEYA

Neyma called, and that ruined what had so far been a pretty good morning.

"So what's that thing you keep doing?" she asked toward the end of the conversation.

"W-what thing?" Kaeya answered.

"You know. That thing you do, with your face? We were talking about it at break today."

We were talking about it? Kaeya's heart sank. People had noticed the tics. Of course they had. Who wouldn't? She was a fool to think she could hide them.

She said something about having to do homework and hung up.

This will blow over, she consoled herself. *Just keep pushing forward.*

THATCHER

The Kelly garage was separate from the house, a few steps from the kitchen door. He hadn't stepped inside the dark and cluttered tomb in forever. It was too full of junk to park the cars in...and too full of Dad, from back in the time when the word actually meant something. But he needed to think, and his noisy Saturday-morning house was not the place for it.

He flipped on the garage's lone light bulb and ventured into abyss.

Like a long-forgotten crime scene, his father's fingerprints were everywhere. On the toolboxes stuffed so full that the lids wouldn't close. On the boxes of seventies-era baseball cards perched precariously on teetering plastic shelves. On the wheel-less 1959 Mustang sitting on blocks in the oil-stained center.

Thatcher ran his fingers along the side of the car's rusty hulk and remembered the zillion hours he'd spent here watching his dad endlessly tinker with the fuel pump, or radiator, or whatever else had captured his dad's attention on a given day.

Dad would go on and on about how he was going to restore the car, paint it blue, with flames on the side like a Hot Wheel. He was going to drive Thatcher to school in it, making him "the coolest kid in Corona."Thatcher daydreamed those words, through first, second, and third grade, all the way until a rainy day in sixth, when it had suddenly dawned on him that he was *walking* to school, not driving in a "cool-looking" Mustang. Not driving because the car was still up on blocks in the garage, where it had rotted away for years. And at that moment, it had dawned on him that he'd never ride in that Mustang. Nobody would. Because his father's words were only feelings, dreams that evaporated when someone tried to touch them.

He grabbed a torn lawn chair from the top of an old bed frame and sat down next to the decaying heap. And he wondered...were his father's wedding vows the same as the Mustang proclamations, feelings splattered across a page like cheap ketchup?

The garage door creaked open, allowing a single ray of light to sneak in. It was Scout. She held one of Mom's old Barbies in one hand and a beat-up-looking

Ken in the other. She pulled an old patio chair cushion from inside her old crib and plopped down next to Thatcher on the floor.

"Whatcha doin?" she said as Barbie sat on Thatcher's armrest.

"Just thinking about stuff," he answered.

"Oh," she said as she made the doll slide down to the ground, arms raised as if she was on an imaginary roller coaster.

He suddenly noticed how much Scout looked like Mom, freckles and all. And for some reason, that worried him.

"Promise me you'll never fall in love with a loser," he told her as he stared vacantly at the Mustang.

"Fall in love? Gross!" she assured as she dropped Barbie on the cement and stared at the car with him.

Thatcher tussled her hair and secretly hoped that her words would last, that she'd always think that love was gross, that she'd stay away from the heart-piercing stares of boys who only intended to take without giving in return.

"Wanna play Barbies?" she asked, her blue eyes wide in the dim light.

"Okay, but I get to be this guy," Thatcher answered as he reached for an ancient spark plug.

"Nooo," Scout giggled. "You have to be Ken."

Thatcher grabbed Barbie out of Scout's hand and made the spark plug kiss her.

"Oh, Barbie," he said in an exaggerated French accent, "how can you think of Ken when it is I, Sparkplug Man, that you truly love?"

The wild romance between Sparkplug Man and Barbie went on for at least five more minutes, with

Sparkplug bragging about his legendary abs, and Scout laughing so hard that she couldn't talk.

Eventually, the romance ended, and it was time to leave. Tossing the spark plug aside, Thatcher stood and reached for Scout's hand. He pulled her up, and they walked toward the door. It was time to move on from the Mustang and all its faded promises. He shut off the light and stepped outside.

He wouldn't be returning to the garage anytime soon.

8

SUNDAY

KAEYA

"It's your call," her dad had said as she walked out the door, which of course meant "Don't go." To him, church was a thing of the past, a place he went to when Mom was still alive, when he still believed in magic.

But to Kaeya, losing her faith would be like losing a part of mom, one of the parts she loved the most. She hadn't been in a few months, but the week had been a hard one. She needed this.

Not today, God, she prayed as she headed toward the baby room, the soundproof area at the back of the church, where parents with small children could watch alive video feed of the service while their babies played.

As always, the room was loud and chaotic, which was good. The noise meant that she could vocalize and tic without causing a total scene.

Dad hated the fact that she sat there. "You shouldn't have to sit with crying babies!" he'd rant.

"No one's making me sit anywhere," she'd argue.

But now that she was here, alone and awkward, she wondered if he was right. There were a lot of parents here, more than usual. They'd notice.

She sat down on one of the cushioned benches that lined the walls. As soon as she did, her neck twisted in an obvious tic, one of the hundreds that had plagued her all morning.

A frazzled-looking mom began to stare, which made the tics worse.

"*Ha Ha!*" she called as she fought to sit upright.

The mom pressed her lips together as if she were about to say something, then looked away.

"*HA HA!*" Kaeya vocalized again.

Grabbing her diaper bag, the woman motioned for her son, then fled into the main sanctuary.

Several facial tics followed, punctuated by a trio of vocalizations. There were looks of pity from two moms in the corner, while a dad gave an awkward smile. They meant well, most of the people at church did, but the unwanted attention always stung.

Countless psychologists and teachers had told her not to feel guilty when people stared or seemed bothered. "It's their problem, not yours," they'd tell her, and she believed them. But today was different.

Whether it was Neyma's blunt comment on the phone or staying up half the night thinking about Kieran, she didn't know, but she was tired, soul tired, and she didn't know if she could make it through the service.

She bowed her head and wiped a tear.

"We wonder why? Why is there suffering?" preached the pastor from the screen overhead.

Why was the word of the weekend. Why had Thatcher been crucified at the pep rally? Why was Quentin in the hospital? Why did she have TS even though she constantly cried out to God to take it away?

The pastor was passionately attempting to answer his unanswerable questions now, but she wasn't really listening. The tics were getting bad, really bad. So she picked up her purse and headed for the door, her questions left behind at the feet of something bigger than herself.

THATCHER

After a weekend of obsessing, he'd come to a conclusion. She was an impossibility, like an unsolvable calculus equation, and the thought of seeing her tomorrow was making him sick to his stomach.

With the alarm set, Thatcher slid his phone back on his nightstand and fell back onto his pillow.

"To sleep, perchance to dream," he whispered. Shakespeare, Hamlet, the death scene, the last line he remembered before falling asleep.

KAEYA

It was Sunday night already. Was Kieran gonna text? She hadn't heard from him since Friday night's textathon, and she already missed him.

She thought of texting him herself, but everything was so new. She didn't want to seem stalkerish.

She looked over at her phone for the millionth time. Nothing.

"Why do you keep checking your texts?" asked Mr. Garay as he flipped off the TV. They'd been watching way too many reruns of *Saved by the Bell*, and it was time for bed.

"It's nothing," Kaeya said as she grabbed her phone and dropped it into the pocket of her pj's.

"Oh, is *Nothing* his name?" he joked as he grabbed the empty bowl of popcorn and walked toward the kitchen.

Kaeya turned red. Was it that obvious?

"I take that as a yes?" he called.

She'd always been honest with him, and it was already out there, so...what the heck.

"Yeah, I've met someone," she said, trying to sound casual.

She regretted the words—*I've met someone*—the second they fell out of her mouth. Now they were all over the floor, and her father was sifting through them like a crazed archeologist.

"Oh," he said after a long pause. "What's his name?" He was nervous, but holding back. Kaeya could tell.

"Kieran. And he plays soccer." The soccer part was on purpose, to appease her dad, who was fanatical about the sport, but not so fanatical about his baby girl having a boyfriend.

Her dad didn't say anything for a while. For a long while. "Does he know?" he eventually said as he walked back into the living room.

Kaeya played with a loose thread on her quilt, wrapping it around her finger like a tiny noose. "Dad, why does that even matter?"

"Preciosa, whether you like it or not, your Tourette's *is*..." Her father stopped midsentence. He'd said too much, and now he felt guilty. After sixteen years, Kaeya could read him like the Jane Austen novels she'd practically memorized.

"Dad, I get it," she answered. "One day Kieran and everyone else in the world will have to know, and the laws of gravity will come crashing down on my messed-up little head. But not yet. I need to enjoy floating weightless for a while. Okay?"

He gave her that look, the *you're making a huge mistake,* and *I have no choice but to let you make it* look.

And she hugged him to show him they were okay.

Her dad went to bed, but she waited through another *Saved by the Bell* episode until she couldn't keep her eyes open anymore. Then, just as she was about to fall asleep. It came.

Saw Quentin today. Sore but smiling.

Kaeya waited a few seconds to text back. *Yay!*

It was going to be a good week.

9

MONDAY

THATCHER

Students were staring as he walked toward the Gallery. Of course they were. What else would they be doing? Now that his meme had topped a million views, he was a celebrity, like Star Wars Kid or Grumpy Cat. Oh yeah, and he was unstable too. He'd hurt someone. Remember?

It wasn't like anyone laughed in his face or joked out loud. That only happened in the movies. They would do their joking behind his back, and that was what bothered him the most.

KAEYA

There was a group of girls next to the vending machine. They watched her as she passed. Were they some of the girls who had noticed her tics? She had no idea, and that was what bothered her the most.

Thatcher

Thatcher had been alone for the first hour of the day, but now that Kaeya was here, the room was full.

"She basically just gave me my independent study work and left," he said. "I mean, where does she go all day?"

"I don't know. Meetings and stuff, I guess," answered Kaeya, who was sitting cross-legged on the green sofa, with a stick of red licorice in her hand.

"Meetings about what?"

"I don't know. Just meetings."

"So she doesn't teach anymore?"

"Well, sort of. She'll teach a random lesson every once in a while."

There was a lull in the conversation as Kaeya got back to her AP econ flowcharts. Except for a few facial tics, she wasn't twitching all that much, and Thatcher wondered why. Did her TS turn off and on? Were some days worse than others? Kaeya was a new novel, and he wanted to discover every line.

She looked busy, so Thatcher got back to his work. He'd shuddered when Mrs. DeGeau gave him the pile. There were hundreds of math problems, reading pages, and an avalanche of Spanish worksheets. His teachers had laid it on, punishment for his misdeeds, he guessed.

"So what kind of lessons does she teach you guys?" he blurted in an attempt to keep the embers of conversation glowing. "I mean, it's not like this is a specific class or anything."

Kaeya put her book down, a good sign.

"Um, it kind of depends," she said. "There was this girl here for a while, with chronic pain issues. For her, it was a lesson on Jackson Pollock."

"He's the guy who splashed pain all over the place, right?" asked Thatcher before taking a sip of the lukewarm hot chocolate.

"Yup, and that's pretty much what we did. Mrs. DeGeau covered the floor with white butcher paper, and we dripped paint all over the place all day. Oh yeah, and then we..." Kaeya was laughing now, so hard that she couldn't finish.

"Sounds like fun," added Thatcher, giggling himself.

"Each time we splattered paint, we had to *state our inner pain*. None of us even knew what that meant. Sam kept saying something like, 'It's so dark inside!' I guess the lesson freaked Chronic Pain Girl out, because she never came back."

And then they laughed until their sides ached and their thoughts calmed to a blissful blue.

"Don't worry. Your project is coming next. Just wait," Kaeya said as she kicked his leg with her stripe-socked right foot.

"Can't wait." He smiled as he toe-tapped her back.

KAEYA

Awesome day. Lunch with Neyma and some of her friends. No tics. Talked to Kieran a little on the way back. Nothing serious, but no tics. Made it through humanities.

Only a few face issues. A day like this was rare, like finding a T. rex fossil in your backyard rare, and she was ecstatic.

Now that she was back at the Gallery for sixth period study hall, she could hardly sit still.

With Mrs. DeGeau humming at her desk, Sam writing away on his laptop in a far corner, and Thatcher sitting and reading across from her, the room was quiet, too quiet.

Tossing her chem book aside, she curled up on the sofa and glanced up at Thatcher. "Whatcha reading?" she asked.

Thatcher looked up. "Oh, believe me—you don't want to know."

"Try me?"

"It's a story about this little kid named Doodle who's really sick and not expected to live. His brother totally resents the fact that Doodle can't play with him and stuff, so he forces him to work out all the time. Totally depressing."

"*The Scarlet Ibis*!" Kaeya laughed.

"Show some respect," he joked. "The little guy's in the middle of *burying* his dead bird."

"Just wait," answered Kaeya. "It gets worse."

"No! Don't tell me Doodle is going to—"

"Yup, just like the bird."

"No, no, no! Not Doodle!" he pleaded.

"That story pretty much damaged me for life." She twirled a strand of her hair and laughed again. She loved laughing. It kept the tics away.

"Why do language arts teachers torture us like this?" Thatcher shook his head an smiled. Her laugh was contagious.

"It's a state standard. *All literature must be depressing.* Have you read *Gift of the Magi* yet?"

"Yeah, in eighth grade. Ruined Christmas forever."

When the laughter died down, she grabbed her math book and calculator out of her backpack and pretended to work on her calculus homework. But she couldn't concentrate.

She tossed the book aside. "Once, when I first got here, Mrs. D assigned us this list of stories to read," she said, breaking the silence.

"Let me guess. *Flowers for Algernon?* Or maybe something happier, like *Heart of Darkness*," he said as he placed his lit book on the coffee table and leaned in.

"No, happy stories. And for the entire week she played songs like "Don't Worry Be Happy" and "It's a Wonderful World." Then we had to create portraits of ourselves out of words cut from magazines. We could only use the *calm* words."

Kaeya looked around, as if she were about to reveal some huge secret. "I'm pretty sure the project was for Sam," she whispered. "You know why he's in here, right?"

Thatcher shook his head no.

"Chronic panic attacks," she said, her tone suddenly turning serious. "They let him come in here to calm down when he's stressed."

"Really? But he seems so chill."

Kaeya picked up a blue-and-white pillow and hugged it. "Exactly. The thing is, Sam says he's faking it."

"No way. You can't fake something like that?"

"I know, right? But that's what he told me. He says he acts stressed so he can work on his screenplay. The guy's obsessed with that thing. Said he got the idea from *Catch 22*."

Thatcher's eyes lit up. "Yossarian, the guy who faked being sick so he could get out of battle," he said. "How's he getting away with it?"

"I know. I can see him fooling his parents, but not the school psych. She's pretty smart."

"Do you believe him?"

She looked over at Sam. He was still wearing headphones, and oblivious to the world. "I'm not sure," she said.

The topic eventually ran out of steam, and they both got back to work. But every once in a while, she'd notice Thatcher looking over at her. And for some reason, she became overly self-conscious—of her vintage polka-dot leggings, her Brooklyn T-shirt, the two braids she hardly ever wore. And that surprised her. Because Thatcher wasn't Kieran.

10

TUESDAY

THATCHER

"Alrighty then!" called Mrs. DeGeau as she feverishly grabbed scattered pieces of notebook paper from her desk.

"Here it comes," whispered Kaeya.

Thatcher set his math book down and stared as Mrs. D danced over to Sam and yanked off his headphones.

"Gather around, my disciples!" she sang as she headed for the sofa.

Sam reluctantly followed her to the center circle, sitting on the armrest of a plush purple chair while Kaeya scooted over on the sofa to make room.

Mrs. D beamed. "I'm a genius, and you will love me for this!"

"Do tell," said Kaeya, who was smiling politely even though they were about to be assigned another project.

"Okay, wait for it...Fifteen Minutes of Fame!" beamed the teacher.

"So you finally made it onto that reality TV show you've been dreaming of," teased Sam.

"Very funny, Mr. Park," she replied. "But you are mistaken. Fifteen Minutes of Fame is the name I've given

Thatcher's character education project, in honor of Thatcher's current notoriety among the denizens of cyberspace."

There it was. The meme again. And she actually used the word cyberspace. Seriously?

"I warned you," said Kaeya, who seemed to be enjoying Thatcher's obvious discomfort.

"I'm sure you've all heard of the phrase 'fifteen minutes of fame.'" Mrs. D continued. "It was a phrase coined by pop artist Andy Warhol in the 1960s."

Thatcher had. The quote was way overused.

"The phrase first appeared in a program for an art exhibition in Stockholm. Warhol's actual words were, 'In the future everyone will be famous for fifteen minutes,'" she lectured. "Do any of you know what it means?"

He had a few theories but decided to keep his mouth shut, like everyone else in the room.

"Warhol meant that in the future, virtually anyone will be able to become famous, whether they deserve it or not."

Mrs. D paused for dramatic effect, staring intently at the blank faces before her. "Well, don't you get it?" she finally said. "Because of social media, Warhol's future is now."

Like a college professor, she stood and circled the sofas. "Nowadays, absolutely anyone can achieve fame, for posting a video of their cat playing a keyboard, for swallowing spoons full of cinnamon." She stopped in front of Thatcher. "For being the subject of a meme."

The room was silent. Was he supposed to say something? Do something? He had no idea.

"Thatcher," she eventually continued, "whether you like it or not, you're *famous*."

She was right. He was famous. For being a loser. And he didn't appreciate the fact that Mrs. D was bringing it up in front of Kaeya.

Mrs. DeGeau suddenly lowered her voice. "Don't worry, my friend. This fame, it's temporary, like a morning mist that disappears with the sun. See, Warhol's words were a warning. We have only fifteen minutes of fame in life...to make a difference."

"Wow, Mrs. D," joked Kaeya as she sat back on the sofa. "Inspiring, completely depressing and futile, but inspiring."

Mrs. D laughed as she handed each of them a paper with *Fifteen Minutes of Fame* scrawled across the top and nothing more. Thatcher was confused, and from the perplexed looks Sam and Kaeya were giving each other, so was everyone else.

Kaeya giggled and shook her head. "Good luck, Thatch," she whispered as she buried her face in her hands.

"So, um, what am I supposed to do?" asked Thatcher.

Mrs. D smiled, as if confusion was her ultimate goal. "Anything you want, of course."

Thatcher ran his hands through his hair as Kaeya and Sam tried hopelessly to stifle their laughter. "Anything?"

"Yes, anything. The blank page is a figurative representation of your life, and you may do whatever you want with it."

Kaeya, who had stopped laughing now, tried to help. "Okay? So you're telling him that he can choose his own character education project?"

"No, I'm telling *all of you* to choose your own character education project."

"Wait, wait, wait," interrupted Sam. "All of us?"

"Yes, the *three* of you. For the next fifteen days, I want you to do something significant with your lives, something huge, something that will make a lasting dent in the sphere of your world."

"But I'm not the one who's suspended," Sam argued.

"No, but you are enrolled in my sixth-period study hall class, and this will be worth 75 percent of your grade. You didn't think you could hang out in my class whenever you feel like it without doing any work, did you?"

It was obvious that she'd made the 75 percent thing up on the spot, like everything else she did.

"You've got to be kidding," mumbled Sam.

"Nope. Not kidding. And your ideas are due tomorrow."

"Oh, come on. It'll be fun," said Kaeya, who was already scribbling away on a sheet of notebook paper.

Sam grabbed a pillow and heaved it at Kaeya's head. She returned the favor.

Oblivious to the cotton-filled projectiles, Mrs. D picked up her book bag and headed for the door. "By the way," she called before exiting, "this is a collaborative project, so I expect you to work together. Make sure to exchange phone numbers."

Thatcher began to panic. "Mrs. DeGeau! Wait!" he called. "I don't really get what we're supposed to do."

She smiled. "You'll figure it out."

KAEYA

Kaeya flipped through the latest Youtopia catalogue while her dad watched soccer on TV. She loved that store. Practically everything it sold was totally unique, especially the dresses.

As for the project, it didn't bother her. She'd think of something. Besides, Mrs. D was an easy grader. Anything she turned in would be good enough.

"See anything you like?" said her father as he passed a bowl of popcorn over.

"Yeah, everything," answered Kaeya as she grabbed a handful. "Way too expensive though."

"Christmas is coming. Put it on your list."

"No, Dad. You don't get it. I'm talking *you need to get a second job to buy a T-shirt there* expensive."

"Mmm," mumbled her father as he turned back to the TV.

Kaeya eyed a vintage-looking light-blue dress on page7—$450. There was no way Santa could afford that.

As she turned the page, her phone vibrated on the coffee table. A text. Kieran!

More Saved by the Bell?

Kaeya smiled. *So what do you have against Zach and Screech?* she typed. But before she could finish, Kieran texted again.

Worried about the calc test. Help me!!!

Help him? This was getting interesting. She stared down at the phone as yet another text arrived.

Friday? LuLu's? I'll buy you a caramel latte.

No way! It was actually happening. Kieran was asking her out! She took a deep breath and basked in the firelight warmth of the moment.

Her father looked over. "Everything all right?" he asked.

"Yeah, perfect," she answered in a daze as she cradled her phone.

LuLu's was cozy and creative, and hanging out there with Kieran would be utterly amazing. But could she do this? Actually survive an entire date with Kieran without him noticing her Tourette's?

Kaeya fingered the numbers on her phone. And suddenly she felt strong, stronger than she had in years. She could do this. And she would. And she would do more than coffee. She would go to Lanterns with him, in a Youtopia dress, and dance until the last song faded away. There were details, of course. There always were. But all she had to do now was type.

What time?

THATCHER

Thatcher liked sharp crayons, and green was the only sharp color left. So he colored the unicorn green. Scout wasn't too happy about that and was making it very clear as she colored the Cutie Bears on the page next to his.

"Thatch, stop!" she repeated for the third time as she pulled the crayon out of his fingers. "Unicorns are supposed to be white."

"Yeah, but white won't show on the white background, so give me the crayon back." Reluctantly, Scout complied.

When the green unicorn was finished, he scribbled in the clouds, a poem by Langston Hughes.

Scout wasn't too happy about having words in the sky either, but Thatcher couldn't help it. Kaeya was figurative language come to life, and every time he thought of her, he remembered why he loved poetry. And now, because of Mrs. D's bizarre project, he had her phone number!

When his sister finally went to bed, he thought of checking on *Marry Me Martha*. But as he picked up his phone, he decided not to. For the first time in a while, he'd had a good day, and he didn't want anything to ruin it.

11

KAEYA

She'd missed calc that morning because she'd been vocalizing like crazy, which also meant she missed Kieran, which was absolutely nerve racking since she had no idea what time their date was. Why hadn't he responded to her last text?

Kaeya thought about texting him again, but decided against it. Too desperate. They still had two days to connect.

Putting her phone away, she entered the Gallery and tried to focus on Sam, who was discussing his *Fifteen Seconds of Fame* project idea with Mrs. D. He seemed excited.

"It's just a trailer for the film, not the actual thing, so I think I can shoot it in a couple of days," he explained as he held up a storyboard. "I'll need to edit and add the soundtrack and stuff, but postproduction shouldn't take too long."

"And where do you plan on premiering this masterpiece?" Mrs. D said as she jotted something down in her journal.

"IndieWire on YouTube," he answered.

"Great," Mrs. D said as she raised her hands in victory. "One thing though. It is a collaborative project. Have you thought about how you're going to incorporate your two friends here?"

"Um, yeah. I was thinking maybe they could act in the trailer...if they want.""Totally!" exclaimed Kaeya. "That...*HA!*...sounds like fun."

"Yeah sure," Thatcher agreed, albeit reluctantly.

She looked over at him as he sipped his hot chocolate. He'd been pretty quiet all morning, and she was curious. What was he thinking about?

Thatcher

Thatcher felt sick to his stomach. Except for a handful of fragmented ideas, he had no idea what to tell Mrs. D.

He tapped his foot on the concrete as Mrs. D finished talking to Sam. Would he have to go next?

Luckily, Mrs. D's cell phone rang. More time to think! Thatcher sifted through his mental files. He figured he could do something with literature since he was always reading. But he didn't know what.

"No, I can't be there until after three," Mrs. D argued into the phone.

Could he turn in one of his quote journals? That would be easy.

"Look, I have to go. I'm in class," she said.

No, the journals wouldn't be good enough. Mrs. D probably wanted something specific.

Mrs. D looked irritated as she put her phone away and headed back to the circle. It was time, and he wasn't ready.

KAEYA

Mrs. D called on Kaeya next. She was ready. She'd been ready for years.

"Ms. Garay," Mrs. D announced. "What are you going to do with your fifteen minutes of fame?"

"You said we could do anything, right?" Kaeya asked. Her face curled up in another tic.

"That's right," assured Mrs. D with a nod.

"And it's totally up to us?"

"Yes."

"Okay, I'm going to Lanterns with Kieran Summerlin. That's my project."

The teacher tapped her chin with her pencil. "I'm not sure I understand."

Kaeya paused and wondered how much she should say.

"It's like this," she began. "I don't need fifteen minutes of fame. I know that'll never...Ha! Ha!...happen. All I need is one dance, at Lanterns, with Kieran. That's all."

Mrs. D reached over and squeezed Kaeya's hand. She looked worried now, just like her dad looked when she told him she wanted to transfer. "But has Kieran even asked you to it yet?"

"No, but we're going out this Friday."

She thought of Kieran's text, or lack of a text, and wondered if the date was even on anymore.

"Well, that's a start," Mrs. D said with a forced smile.

Kaeya's eyes were tearing up. She bit her lip to shake it off.

Just then, the phone rang again. "Grrrr! My husband again," she grumbled as she headed outside.

With Mrs. D gone, the room fell into an awkward silence.

"Fifteen seconds," Thatcher finally said, his words soft.

"What?" she asked.

"All you're asking for is fifteen seconds…fifteen seconds of Normal."

And for the first time in months, she started to cry.

THATCHER

Thatcher had let his heart get away from him, like the balloon he let go at Disneyland when he was five. This definitely felt worse.

For over a week, he'd been in this happy state of denial, ignoring the name Kieran like he would ignore a fly. But the denial had worn out, and now his heart hurt, physically ached.

Kaeya wanted Kieran, not him. She was going out with Kieran on Friday. And now all that was left of life was a broken home and a social life in ruins.

He wanted to leave, to run out of the room toward anywhere. But it was his turn.

"Thatcher. Your project?" Mrs. D said.

"Oh, I was thinking of collecting quotes and putting them in a journal," he said, improvising. He knew it wouldn't be enough, but at least it was something.

"What kind of quotes?"

"Uh, literary quotes. You know, Dickens, Jules Verne, and..." He'd collected quotes from a million authors, but with Kaeya staring at him, he was drawing a blank.

Mrs. D snapped her fingers as if she was trying to conjure up the right words, and when they came, she sat forward in her seat and smiled. "Allow me to rephrase the question. What *kind* of quotes? As in, what will the quotes be about?"

Thatcher drew a blank. "I'm...I'm not sure."

"Okay, I can help with that. What have you been concerned about lately?"

The question seemed personal, too personal. But Mrs. D looked like the kind of person who wouldn't loosen her grip until she'd extracted the answers she wanted. So he gave her what she wanted.

"So, my dad left my mom last week. And then they took my picture. And now the whole world is laughing at the picture, at me."

"And you've been wondering about?"

"About how uncool people can be, and about the complete lack of love in the world, I guess," he answered.

Mrs. D practically jumped out of her seat with excitement. "Good. Go on. What about love?"

"Um, it's like I've been getting so many messages about what love isn't that I'm forgetting what love actually *is*."

The words surprised him, as if his soul had conspired an answer without him.

"I understand. So, you'll collect quotes about love then. And how will these quotes change the world?"

"I guess I can post them on a website or something. That way people can read them."

"That's a start!" said Mrs. D. "'Words read and forgotten are wasted ink on paper, but words acted upon become monuments.'"

Thatcher recognized the quote from *The Waiting*, Lionel Barnes, 1936.

"But there must be more you can do," she continued. "Come on, Thatcher. Over a million people have seen your meme. You have an audience. So speak!"

Thatcher bit his lip. He had no desire to become an online street preacher.

"Ooooh! I got it," said Kaeya. "How about you post pictures of yourself holding up quotes like you did in the quad that day? Only this time the quotes can be about love, and tolerance, and stuff like that."

"*Yes!*" cried his teacher. "And by doing so you can rewrite the narrative."

Thatcher didn't like where this was going. He wanted *Marry Me Martha* to go away, not turned into some national anti-bullying campaign.

"Yeah, and you can recreate the meme," blurted Sam. "You know, dress exactly like you did on the day of the picture, mess up your hair, everything. That way people will think it's another *Marry Me Martha* picture. They'll pay more attention that way."

"Oh, I'm getting goose bumps!" said Mrs. D as she held her arms out. "It reminds me of Artur Fontanbleau's modern art exhibit at the Pompidou Centre in Paris. He had videos of negative media images, and then he counteracted them by showing the simplicities of everyday life."

Kaeya got up and sat next to him, *right* next to him. "You should do it, Thatcher," she encouraged. "It'll be like fighting back, with words."

Recreating a meme that had practically destroyed his life was stupid—no, more than stupid. It was insane.

Kaeya was so close he could smell her gum, strawberry. "Come on. I'll help you," she said as she reached over and messed up his hair.

That was enough to steer him off the cliff.

"All right," he whispered.

KAEYA

She thought about Thatcher on the drive home, how he reminded her of the guy from that band, Falling Up. He had the same high cheekbones and hair. He even dressed like the guy: V-neck, open cardigan, ripped jeans.

He'd told her about Tolstoy that afternoon, how he gave up all his riches to live like a peasant. Thatcher was a good storyteller. Maybe one day they could hang out, as friends.

But not this week. She had a date to go on, if she ever figured out when it was.

THATCHER

Thatcher pulled on the T-shirt. It smelled. It was wrinkled. It looked stupid, totally stupid.

He leaned his phone at eye level on the bookshelf, set the timer, and held up the quote.

If everyone isn't beautiful, then no one is.

Andy Warhol. An ironic choice, considering the dude was a pacifist, and the picture Thatcher was about to take was a declaration of war.

The phone clicked, and it was over. At least for now, in the late-night minutes before morning, before the world would see.

He stared at the image and momentarily panicked. Why was he doing this? That school picture had ruined his life, ruined everything. And now he was trying to re-create it?

The answer was difficult and easy all at once. It was Shakespeare, and Dickens, and a million other writers who had inspired him with their words. It was anger, and inspiration, and an insatiable desire to rewrite the narrative and become something better. For Kaeya. The Ghost. The girl who appeared and vanished like a morning mist...the girl he was beginning to love.

Yes, she liked Kieran, and that hurt. But he'd decided. He would love her anyway, even if there was nothing in it for him.

KAEYA

Kaeya stared down at the text for the millionth time. *Is seven okay?*

It was happening, really happening.

She sat up on her bed and imagined walking into LuLu's on Friday night. The coffee place would be packed and noisy, as always. She'd see him sitting toward the back. He'd look up and smile, and she'd smile back. And that was as far as she could imagine. Because going on a first date with Kieran Summerlin was a mystery, a blissful mystery, one that would give her nightmares.

Suddenly, she panicked. Why had she texted yes? Kieran would find out, for sure. LuLu's was small, and he'd be close, close enough to notice.

She was terrified, but excited. Mostly excited. Well, maybe mostly terrified. She couldn't really tell due to an extreme case of Kieran-induced insomnia. She liked him, more than liked him. And for the first time in forever, she felt confident that a guy—a perfect, *straight out of an H&M ad* looking guy—might actually like her back.

She had Thatcher to thank for that, Instagram Thatcher, the one who'd accidentally stumbled upon her hiding place and discovered her heart, discovered and didn't mind.

12

KAEYA

It was way too early for the Gallery. Kaeya usually made a point of avoiding it until at least after ten. But today was different. She needed to rest up for calculus. She wanted to connect with Kieran about Friday.

Thatcher had his headphones on as he sat at his usual spot on the sofa. He had no idea that she'd walked in.

She couldn't resist. With the stealth of a ninja, she tiptoed behind him, pulled off his headphones, and screamed, "Zombie attack!"

"Whaaaat!" yelled Thatcher as he threw his book across the room and fell onto the floor.

Feeling guilty, she immediately ran over to help him up.

"Okay, zombies don't scream 'zombie attack!' when they're about to kill someone." He smiled as he waved his hands in the air like *I'm totally fine, and that wasn't embarrassing at all*, a move that Kaeya didn't believe since his face was beet red.

She was laughing now, hysterically, and could barely squeeze out the words. "Would you have preferred that I killed you without warning?"

"Yes, please," he said. "I'd rather not know when I'm about to die."

Thatcher was laughing as he walked over to where his science book was sprawled across the floor. She didn't feel so guilty anymore.

"You're early," he said as he picked the book up and flipped through its pages.

"Yeah, I can't miss third period today."

Kaeya followed Thatcher back to the sofa—*his* sofa, the purple one—and for some reason sat next to him instead of taking her usual spot across the table. He didn't seem to mind.

"Kieran's in that class. Right?"

"Yup."

"One more day," said Thatcher as he opened the book on his lap. "You nervous?"

"A little. I guess."

"You'll do great."

"Thanks. By the way, we need to meet up for Sam's movie."

Thatcher pushed his book aside, the one he wasn't really reading. "Sure, what day works for you?"

"Well, today's out because I'm leaving school early for my monthly *counseling* session." She rolled her eyes. "Don't even get me started about that."

"Well, just let me know. My schedule's pretty open."

"Sam says tomorrow works. How about my house after school?"

"But what about your date?"

"That's later. We can get a couple of hours of filming in before then."

"All right. Friday after school it is," said Thatcher.

"I'll confirm with Sam and get back to you. I've been texting him all morning, but he's not answering. Probably daydreaming about movies. The guy's obsessed."

Thatcher pulled a folder out of his backpack. "Is his screenplay any good?" he said.

"I have no idea, but I guess we'll find out."

Thatcher nodded quietly and got back to work. She liked that about Thatcher, the way he didn't feel the need to fill the air with words. He made her feel comfortable.

They worked side by side for over an hour, occasionally looking up at each other to make a comment about Mrs. D or US history or whatever. When she finally looked at the clock, third period was about to start. Unzipping her backpack, she began packing her books. It was Kieran time.

Kaeya realized that her hands were sweating, and that wasn't good. More stress meant more tics. She stopped packing and took a deep breath, then another. It didn't work. She was starting to tic again, not bad, but enough to worry her. She was going to class, no matter what. She grabbed her backpack and stood. Thatcher stood, and they walked to the door together.

"Kaeya," he said as he tapped her forearm. "It's gonna work out."

"I know," she answered, feigning confidence. "I'll call you tonight...about Friday."

"See ya," he answered as she walked away.

She opened the door, and a blast of cold air rushed into the room. She looked back and saw him standing at the door. The Gallery was warm, and she wished she could stay.

THATCHER

Mrs. D was back, and so was her music, Italian opera this time. She hadn't mentioned the project, which was good since Thatcher was actually thinking about deleting his first post.

He crumpled his granola bar wrapper and basketballed it into the nearest wastebasket.

"Three points," called Sam, who was sitting across from him.

"Yup," Thatcher answered as he stood and stretched. He'd been laboring over calculus all morning and was going stir crazy without Kaeya to talk to.

"So Kaeya said you're into movies?" Thatcher asked as he sat back down.

"Yeah," Sam said softly, so softly that Thatcher had to lean in to hear. He looked like he was having trouble breathing, and Thatcher wondered whether he should just leave him alone.

"Cool," he answered.

Sam's weird breathing continued, like he *really* was about to have a panic attack. Thatcher looked over at Mrs. D, who was presently closing her eyes in an opera-induced trance. Should he let her know?

"So what's the best film of all time?" Thatcher asked when the music mellowed.

Sam looked up from his laptop. "Are you talking modern or classic?"

"Um, I don't know. Both, I guess."

"Modern era, *Forrest Gump*, for sure."

"Life's a box of chocolates," added Thatcher, who'd seen the movie at least three times.

"It's actually 'Mama always said life was like a box of chocolates,' but close enough." Sam flipped closed his laptop and took another deep breath. "As for black-and-white films—*Casablanca*."

"Haven't seen it," Thatcher said.

"Are you kidding me? Dude, Humphrey Bogart and Ingrid Bergman. It's one of the greatest films of all time." Sam was excited now. "You know that line 'Play it again, Sam'?"

Thatcher nodded as if he'd heard it, but had no idea what Sam was talking about.

"I'm named after that guy," he said. "Sam, the piano player."

"So your parents named you after a character in *Casablanca*? No wonder you're so into movies."

"Actually, I picked Sam myself...when I moved from Korea. My parents thought my name was too hard to pronounce, so they told me to choose an American one."

"What's your real name?"

"Park Min-Jun."

"That's not that hard to pronounce."

"My dad thought so. He wanted me to assimilate with the culture."

Mrs. D was singing along with the aria now, and they both turned to look.

"Sam was, like, the coolest character," Sam said. "The dude's world is falling apart, and he keeps on playing his piano like World War II was a figment of everyone's imagination."

"Was it hard losing your name? I mean, it's kind of part of who you are."

Sam thought about it for a few seconds. "Yeah, but I was only ten, so I didn't really realize it. I was just happy to be going to America. I thought that things would be different here, like in all the movies."

"Different? Like how?"

"You know, happier. My dad worked all the time in Korea, and I thought we'd get to see him more once we moved. But *that* never happened."

Sam suddenly looked sad, and Thatcher regretted asking about the whole name thing. He tried to change the subject. "Hey, did Kaeya talk to you about filming tomorrow?"

"Yeah. We're on."

"Cool." Thatcher rummaged through his backpack for something to do. He couldn't find anything, so for the next hour he daydreamed about watching *Casablanca* with Kaeya.

KAEYA

Third period was over, and students were still filing out of the room. Kieran was up front, talking to Ms. Candele about a missing assignment. Should she wait for him? No, too stalker-like. Frustrated, she picked up her bag and headed for the door. She'd made it through class, the entire stupid class, but they hadn't talked. Of course, with her getting to class late and Ms. Candele going over the study guide all period, they didn't really get the chance.

Making matters worse, her brain was starting to misfire. "Ha! Ha!" she blurted as she reached the glass double doors.

Should she even attempt fourth period? No, her counseling session was in forty-five minutes. She pushed open the doors and headed toward the office to check out.

But as she reached the cement stairs of the math building, she heard someone.

"Where are you off to in such a hurry?" Kieran said casually as he trotted up to her. Kaeya wondered if he'd heard her vocalize. From the smile on his face, she didn't think so.

"Ditching Mr. Selznick's class," she joked.

"Oh, that dude is so boring! I had him for AP Euro last year."

"Actually, I have a doctor's appointment." She smiled as she looked at the ground and tried to suppress another vocalization.

Kieran's face grew serious, as if he was avoiding something. "Um, Kaeya, about Friday," he said.

Kaeya's heart sank. Was he about to cancel?

"Our soccer schedule's all messed up because of field maintenance. I tried to connect with you in class yesterday, but you weren't there."

Just rip off the Band-Aid, Kieran. Just get it over with.

"Anyway, I have a game after school tomorrow."

No, no, no. He'd found out about her TS. He *was* cancelling.

"That's okay," she said, trying to mask her disappointment. "Some other time then."

"No, that's not what I meant. Not at all," he assured. "I still wanna hang out. Is eight too late? Or how about this? You go to my game, and we grab something to eat afterwards."

Watch him play? Have dinner? Kaeya wanted to scream YES! at the top of her lungs. But then reality hit. A game, then dinner would take hours. There was no way she could hide her condition for that long.

"Thanks," she said, "but I have this group project I have to work on after school, so the whole dinner thing wouldn't work...but eight's fine. Meet you at LuLu's?"

"Sure, cool," he said softly. For a second, his eyes looked different, and Kaeya wondered. Was he as disappointed about dinner as she was?

THATCHER

Why was he checking his phone again? This Thatcher-loves-Kaeya + Kaeya-loves-Kieran equation was shredding him apart. He needed to remove himself from the formula...but she said she'd call, and the phone was on the desk in front of him, so he checked again.

This is insanity, he thought as he flicked a paper clip off his desk.

There was a knock on his bedroom door. Mom. She looked nervous as she came in and sat on the end of his bed.

"What's up?" he said as he spun his chair around.

"Dad called today," she said, her words slow and careful.

"Okay?" he said.

"He wants to take you and Scout out to dinner."

"When?"

"In like fifteen minutes?" she answered, her face scrunched up as if she knew how ridiculous she sounded.

"But it's totally late!"

"You know he works late sometimes."

"Yeah, having a girlfriend usually keeps a guy pretty busy," he argued.

Mom looked hurt, and Thatcher instantly regretted the words.

"Mom, I already ate. And I'm waiting for a phone call."

"I know it's ridiculously last minute, and awkward given our present situation...but he's your father. Plus, Scout's excited about it."

Thatcher checked the time. Past eight. "It's always about Dad, isn't it? His needs. His schedule."

"Thatcher, don't make this difficult for me. I can't handle difficult right now. Just go," Mom pleaded.

Difficult for her? She wouldn't be the one sitting awkwardly in a restaurant with a father who'd made himself a stranger. But, as always, Thatcher kept quiet. Mom was going through a lot, and he didn't want to make things worse.

"All right," he said, making sure his phone was charged.

KAEYA

The new animal-like vocalizations had been going on for nearly an hour now, and Kaeya wanted more than anything to fall asleep so they'd go away.

"Arrrr! Arrr!" she screamed, this time into her pillow. She felt sorry for her father, who was trying to watch a game, and even more sorry for Sam, whom she'd just got off the phone with. He seemed pretty freaked out when she screamed into the receiver.

The more she ticked and vocalized, the more she worried about Friday, to the point that she felt like throwing up.

This Kieran thing is totally unrealistic, she thought as she headed for the bathroom just in case.

"So how are you going to present your condition to this gentleman?" Dr. Jaya had asked in their session earlier in the day.

"I'm not," she answered.

"And do you think that's realistic?"

"Realistic is overrated," Kaeya had argued. "Movies aren't realistic, and they make billions of dollars. Disneyland isn't realistic, and it's the *happiest place on earth*. So what's so stinkin' bad about being *un*realistic?"

The psychologist had answered with more questions. Which made Kaeya feel more doubtful about her plan than ever. And now, with her head hanging over a toilet, it came to her. She wouldn't last five minutes at LuLu's.

She needed to do something to keep from throwing up...and to keep from giving up. She needed to talk, to someone who knew, someone who would listen.

For some reason, Thatcher came to mind.

THATCHER

Lights were flashing, bells were ringing, and Thatcher had a headache. He hated Eatzalottapizza, hated the whole idea of helping Dad appease his guilt.

He was telling Scout about another pizza place, in San Diego. Of course, it was bigger than this place and had way more games. Scout sat next to him and listened like he was describing the lost city of Atlantis.

"Do they have prizes there?" she asked with excited eyes.

"Oh, totally," Dad answered. "The prizes are actually a lot better than this place. I'll take you there sometime. Maybe next week."

Scout bounced up and down in her chair and clapped. But Thatcher knew it would never happen. San Diego was over two hours away, and Dad would forget the offer by the time he finished his slice of pizza.

"Dad's not taking you anywhere," mumbled Thatcher over the din of the arcade. Scout didn't hear."What?" she asked as she played with the stuffed tiger Dad had won for her in the claw game.

"Never mind," he said as he fiddled with the straw of his Coke.

"Yeah, we'll make a day of it," Dad added, completely oblivious that Thatcher was on to him.

"No, you won't," he said.

"Excuse me?" asked his father.

Thatcher was about to say something, about how most fathers didn't lie to their five-year-old daughters, but instead he stood up. "I'm walking home," he said as he grabbed his sweatshirt off the back of his chair.

"Thatcher, come on. I drove all the way out here to be with you guys. The least you can do is act civil," Dad lectured. But Thatcher wasn't listening.

"He'll get over it. Teenagers are moody like that sometimes," he heard his dad explain to Scout on his way out.

When he reached the parking lot, Thatcher leaned over his knees and screamed. It would take over an hour to walk home, and it was raining, but he was too frustrated to care. He hit the crosswalk button and waited for the signal to change. And that was when his phone vibrated.

He yanked it from his pocket. It was Kaeya.

"Hello," he said coolly as he shivered in the rain.

"Hey," she answered, her voice from somewhere warm.

"Hey, what's up?"

"So Sam says he can meet up after school tomorrow. You good with that?"

"Totally," Thatcher answered, his hands freezing as he clung to the phone. He sounded way too excited. *Tone it down*, he thought.

"Your house. Right?"

"Yup, that's the plan. I live over at West Terrace. You can follow me after school, if you want?"

"S-sure. I'll do that...I mean, if you don't mind," he answered. He wanted to keep her on the phone but had no idea how. "So I guess I'll see you tomorrow then."

His face was starting to feel like an ice block, and his teeth were starting to chatter.

"Are you okay?" Kaeya asked sweetly. "You sound funny."

"I'm fine. Just cold."

"You're not outside, are you? It's freezing."

"Yeah, I'm walking home from Eatzalottapizza. It's kind of a long story."

"I have time," she said softly.

Her voice was warm. Thatcher needed warm.

KAEYA

Kaeya pulled a blanket over her knees as Thatcher explained. It was pouring now—she could hear it hammering the roof, and Thatcher's phone.

"I was with my sister and dad," Thatcher said. He sounded embarrassed.

"And you guys walked all the way to Norco?"

"No, it's just me walking back because I..."

"Because you what?" she asked.

"I guess I just needed to get away from that dancing Eatzalottapizza rat." He was trying to act all happy about it, but Kaeya wasn't buying it.

"So you decided to walk four miles in the rain? Sounds like a serious rodent allergy."

Except for the sound of raindrops, there was silence on the other end of the line. Had she said too much?

"No, um, it's actually my dad I'm allergic to." He paused again.

"You don't get along?"

"Not since he started the whole midlife crisis thing. He's been acting pretty manic lately."

"So what's he crisis-ing about?"

"Well, for one thing, the dude works in a cubicle all day...selling cubicles."

She tried to keep from laughing but failed. "You're kidding right?"

"No, I'm dead serious. It's like he's in that movie *Inception*, only with depressing jobs instead of dreams." Now he was laughing too.

Thatcher changed the subject to pizza, which somehow led to a long conversation about Netflix, which then led to how disorganized Mrs. D always seemed.

Kaeya was getting sleepy, but she fought to stay awake. Thatcher seemed lonely, and she wanted to keep him company.

"Don't feel like you have to stay on the phone with me," he said after one of her yawns.

"It's all right. I'll be your walking buddy," she answered. "So where are you now?"

"Um, over by the Walmart. I think."

"Thatcher, that's crazy far."

"It's not that far. Besides, it's better out here than in my dad's car."

He was lying. It was far. Walmart was probably another hour's walk away from Corona, a wet hour's walk. And from the way his voice sounded, he was freezing.

"So you'd rather be outside in a storm than with your dad?" she said. "That's pretty bad."

"Yeah, I guess. Since you put it that way."

Kaeya heard thunder now. She got out of bed and moved to the window. "So what is it? Are you mad, sad, confused?"

"Check all three."

"Start with confused then," she said, hoping she wasn't scaring him back into his shell.

"There's this picture on our wall, of my mom and dad," he began. "It's from their wedding reception. They're sitting at this table with all these red balloons behind them in the shape of a heart. And in the middle of the heart there's this cheap poster board with the words *Ella and Jake Forever* scribbled on it."

Thatcher stopped talking again, and Kaeya fought the urge to fill the air with words. *All you need to do is listen*, she told herself as she pulled on a sweatshirt.

"I don't know. That poster really bothers me...because it's a lie. Their love wasn't forever, and now I'm starting to wonder if they ever loved each other in the first place. I mean, isn't love, real love, supposed to be more than just words on a poster?"

She fiddled with a loose string on her sweatshirt.

"It is," she said.

"Is what?"

"More than words on a poster. At least I think so."

THATCHER

He'd made it past the sketchy part of town and was halfway home. His sweatshirt and jeans were soaked, and his feet were freezing, but he'd been talking to Kaeya for almost an hour now, so he didn't even notice.

He was about to take a shortcut through the orange groves, when he saw it, a car slowing down behind him. With thoughts of muggers fresh in his mind, he picked up his pace. He was about to break out into a run, but the car pulled up to the curb in front of him and stopped.

Thatcher froze. Should he run back?

"Just get in the car already," he heard a voice call out. It was coming from the phone.

"Oh my gosh! You didn't have to do this!" he said as he ran over to the open window of Kaeya's blue VW Bug. "You're crazy!"

"I'm crazy?" she laughed. "Look at you."

He didn't want to look. He probably looked worse than on meme day.

"Hey, I really appreciate this," he said as he got in. The car was warm. Perfect.

"I figured you needed a hug," she said.

"I doubt you'd want to hug me right now—I'm totally soaked."

She looked over at him and smiled. "Yeah, I think the hug will have to wait."

As they drove on, Thatcher couldn't believe what was happening. He was sitting in Kaeya's car! And the Vogue model–category girl sitting next to him wasn't running away. Insane.

The thought gave him confidence to bring up a sensitive topic, the one that worried him most. "Hey, did you end up talking to Kieran today?" he asked.

"I did actually. We're meeting at LuLu's later now because of his soccer game. But better late than never, right?"

Her words were painful, negating every happy second of the last hour. "You guys'll have fun," he said, trying to sound happy for her, but doing a pretty crappy job.

"I guess," she answered.

She didn't sound very positive about it. Was there a crack in the window? A crack that he could crawl through?

"You guess?" he asked.

"I'm pretty stressed about it."

"Hey, what happened to 'keep your face to the sunshine'?" Thatcher said, remembering a quote she'd shown him in her lit book.

"I know. Helen Keller would hate me. But I'm just worried that Kieran will find out."

For a split second, he was tempted to sabotage the date, to tell her that Kieran would find out...but this wasn't about him and what he wanted. This was about Kaeya. Kaeya, who'd interrupted her night to pick him up. Kaeya, whom he was starting to care about more than himself.

KAEYA

"You know, you could always tell him," Thatcher said. "He'd probably understand. I did."

It sounded like something her dad would say. And then again, it sounded totally different. More hopeful.

"Yeah, he probably would. But then he'd be all nice to me *because* of my TS...and that's what scares me the most."

Her voice cracked a little. *Don't cry*, she told herself.

"I'm sorry. I was lecturing."

"No, it's not that," she said. "I've been crying off and on all night. I just get tired of being me sometimes."

"Me too," he said.

Thatcher told her to turn left at the light. It was quicker that way. But Kaeya didn't want quicker. This driving through the rain, she was enjoying it.

"You know, when I was in elementary school, my TS didn't even bother me that much," she continued. "Every year, the school psychologist would introduce me to my new class and give a lesson about my TS. And after her speech, everyone would want to play with me and stuff. I always felt special, like a rock star.

"But when junior high came around, there were other people there, people that hadn't grown up going to school with me. Every once in a while, I'd see one of them mimicking my facial tics behind my back and laughing and stuff."

"Not cool," Thatcher said.

"Well, yeah, but it was junior high. It comes with the territory."

"Still hurts though."

"I guess, but it was the way my friends were acting that hurt the most. They were still nice to me and stuff, but it was almost like they *knew* they were being nice, as if by hanging out with me, they were doing a good deed."

"Like recycling or fighting global warming."

"Exactly! Then in eighth grade, I got invited to my best friend, Jessica's, birthday party. I looked forward to it for a month. My mom even bought me a new outfit.

When I got there, I noticed everyone acting kind of strange, like they were in on some secret or something. And the entire party was over in like forty-five minutes. We had punch and some cookies, but that was it."

"Weird."

"I know. Right? Well, the next day, I was in language arts making up a quiz, and I overheard a girl talking about Jessica's party out in the hall. Apparently, after the cookies, they'd all gone out to a movie and then dinner...without me."

"What? "Thatcher asked. "That's crazy."

"Not that crazy. I can't go to movies. The last time I went, the manager came up to me with his little flashlight and told me people were complaining. Jessica knew that, so she and her mom had planned a *special* birthday get-together beforehand to be nice."

"And that's when you decided that you wanted to transfer," he said softly.

"Right. But then my mom died at the end of eighth grade, and my father thought I needed to go to a high school where I at least knew people. So I started high school at Centennial...but all along I had this plan, to escape."

"And so you came to Glen."

"Yup, and so far, so good. Sure, some people have probably noticed. But for the most part, I think I've been getting away with. I mean, look. I have a date with Kieran Summerlin. What more could I ask for?"

Thatcher didn't answer. And she wondered. Was his silence an answer in itself?

THATCHER

Kaeya pulled up next to the liquid amber tree. He was home. If this were a date, he would lean over and kiss her, gently, as rain drops echoed off the metal roof. But this wasn't a date, he reminded himself. It was Kaeya being nice to a friend, and that was all.

His heart felt heavy as he unbuckled and reached for the door.

"Thanks *so* much. I totally appreciate this," he told her as he stepped out into the rain. "No problem," she said, putting the car into gear. But just as he was about to shut the door, she stopped.

"Thatcher, this whole *Kieran likes me* thing isn't forever. That would be impossible. But I'm not shooting for forever."

The out-of-the-blue comment seemed random. Why was she bringing this up?

He ducked his head back into the car. "I get it," he said. "It's that whole fifteen seconds of normal thing again. Right?"

"I guess," she answered.

The rain mellowed into a gentle mist, creating circles around street lights. It was beautiful.

"Well, I think you deserve more than fifteen seconds," he added. "A lot more."

KAEYA

Kaeya clicked her lamp off and fell back into the warmth of her comforter. She'd trained herself to think happy thoughts before bed. Worrying about stuff meant more tics, and the tics kept her awake.

Tonight's happy thoughts involved Kieran and how they'd be hanging out tomorrow. She imagined him sitting across the table from her and laughing about something random. He was a dream, and the dream was coming true.

It'll work out, she thought as she turned toward the window and closed her eyes.

She was almost asleep when her thoughts switched to Thatcher, and about how they'd talked for over an hour...and how she hadn't ticked the entire time.

THATCHER

His phone was getting wet as he pointed it down Citrus Park's long stairs but he didn't care. With the tips of his Addidas visible at the bottom of the frame, he made sure the words he'd chalked on the tops of five steps were readable and took the picture.

Love is a cold night, warmed by the voice of a friend.

This time, the quote was his own.

~ 145 ~

13

KAEYA

Kaeya couldn't believe it. She was heading to fifth period. Fifth period! She'd actually lasted all the way through lunch without having to go to the Gallery! Not even once!

Sure, she'd had to take some trips to the bathroom. Okay, lots of trips to the bathroom. But she'd made it to bio!

Even better than that, she'd talked to Kieran in the morning, then in class for a while, and he'd told her they'd talk some more tonight. Tonight! She was going to hang out with him tonight! Her face actually ached from smiling. Why had she doubted her plan? She had this.

A senior walked past carrying flowers and a sign.

Kaeya watched as he disappeared into a classroom. Another Lanterns ask. They'd been going on all week. Maybe Kieran would be asking her soon. It was a huge *maybe*, but she'd actually made it to fifth period, and now anything seemed possible.

THATCHER

Thatcher tried to finish his DBQ essay on the reasons for the Civil War, but he couldn't concentrate.

"She's never this late," Sam said, as if he could read Thatcher's mind. "She's usually in here by at least eleven."

"Who, Kaeya?" Thatcher said, as if he had no idea what Sam was talking about.

"Who else would I be talking about?"

Thatcher, who was in full *I'm not crushing on Kaeya* mode, tried to change the subject. "Hey, toss me the script," he said. "I need to look over my lines for today."

Sam's face lit up as he slid a stapled pack of papers across the coffee table. "Don't worry about memorizing the lines perfectly. You guys can ad lib a little, or a lot, if you want."

"So what's your screenplay actually about?" Thatcher asked as he picked it up.

"It's about these two friends, a guy and a girl, with completely messed-up families. They always dream of running away to Prague in the Czech Republic. For some reason, they think it's like this perfect place. Anyway, they don't have any money, so the guy figures out a way to use his dad's frequent flier miles."

The story sounded cheesy, and it was. In fact, it was the sappiest thing he'd ever read. But he wasn't about to let Sam know.. "Wow. This isn't bad," he lied.

Sam smiled. "Yeah, Kaeya thought so too."

Kaeya. Her name was a melancholy wave. School was almost over, and she was still gone. Of course, she could have been absent...or maybe she'd made it through all her classes. That would be a good thing, right?

He looked up at the clock. It didn't feel like a good thing.

KAEYA

Mrs. D and Thatcher were huddled over an iPad while Sam filmed. Needless to say, it was an odd scene.

"Brilliant!" said Mrs. D. "So what compelled you to choose that particular quote?"

"Um, I don't know. I guess I just kind of liked it?" Thatcher answered.

Kaeya, who'd just arrived, figured they were talking about his project. He must have posted something. She put her bag on the floor and sat next to him.

"Well, it's a perfect word choice. Instead of hating or hurting or getting revenge, you've decided to stick with beauty. Good start!"

Kaeya scooted closer to take a look. Surprisingly, Thatcher's picture looked exactly like the original meme, only his expression was different, calm but defiant at the same time. And starting off with that Warhol quote was clever.

Sam moved in for a close-up, and Mrs. D waved him away.

"Look, you almost have two hundred views already," she said. "How did you manage that?"

"I used the *Marry Me Martha* hashtag, so when people were searching for the original meme, the new one would come up," he said. His eyes, they looked joyful, and joy looked good on him.

"How many views did last night's post get?"

Last night's post? She'd have to remember to look for it later.

"I think it has like five hundred already," he bragged.

Kaeya sat quietly on the purple sofa, listening, until Mrs. D became aware of her presence.

"So how are your fifteen minutes of fame coming along, Miss Garay?" she asked.

Kaeya gave Sam a *You film this, and you die* look. Sam put the camera down.

"Well, I'm going out with Kieran tonight...with the perfect outfit." Kaeya pulled up a picture on her phone and walked over to Mrs. D.

"Long lace shirt over leggings. Ahh-mazing!" said Mrs. D.

"I hope so," Kaeya said as she walked back over to the sofa. She wanted to show Thatcher her outfit, but she didn't want to embarrass him.

Kaeya put her phone in her book bag and sank back onto the sofa. The clock shouted twenty minutes left of school. Tonight she'd be seeing Kieran, and everything was going to work out...somehow.

THATCHER

"Drive slow so I don't lose you," Thatcher said as they walked across the parking lot after school. Sam had left already, the tires of his SUV squealing as he took off.

"Just come with me?" Kaeya asked. "It'll be a lot easier."

Thatcher's pulse raced. Kaeya and him? Driving together again? It took everything to keep from sprinting toward the passenger side door.

"But then you'd have to drive back here again," he said, to be polite.

"It's no big deal. I have to come back here tonight anyway."

Driving back for her date with Kieran, he remembered. Ouch!

"All right," said Thatcher as he watched her get into the light-blue Bug. Now that it was daytime, he noticed how perfectly it matched the color of her eyes.

"This is such a cool car," he commented as he swung into the passenger seat.

"She's forty years old but running like a teenager."

"So it's a she then?"

"Abigail the second, or Abby for short," she said. "My mom had Abigail the first."

He took a deep breath. Everything inside smelled like Kaeya. "How long have you had it, I mean, her?" he asked.

"Since I was thirteen. It was a gift from my mom."

"So your mom was a fan of underage driving?" He immediately regretted the words. Her mother was dead. You weren't supposed to make jokes about dead people.

Kaeya smiled as she pulled out of the parking lot. It was okay.

"When my mom was dying, she'd tell me that I was her favorite movie, and that she didn't want to miss the best parts, like my first day of high school, meeting my first boyfriend, and my wedding."

Thatcher noticed that Kaeya was speeding. She didn't look like the speeding type.

"So on my thirteenth birthday, I wake up and there's this car in the driveway. And Mom says it's for me, and I say, 'But I can't even drive.' Then she says, 'No, but now I won't miss seeing the look on your face when you get your first car.'"

"That's awesome," Thatcher said as he hung on to the dashboard.

"I know, and that wasn't all. Over the next few weeks, she took me to my first day of high school, even though I was still in eighth grade. We took pictures in front of the gate, which was pretty awkward. We even went shopping for prom dresses, just for fun."

"So did you re-create your wedding day too?" Thatcher added.

"No, she wasn't that weird." She laughed. "But we basically covered everything else. Well, except for tonight."

"Your first date," Thatcher realized. "I'm so sorry, Kaeya."

"I am too," she answered.

They drove in silence for a few minutes, until they reached the freeway.

"I hope you guys have an awesome time," Thatcher finally said. And he meant it.

KAEYA

Sam had already filmed the scene three times, each from a different angle, but he was a perfectionist, so he wanted to film it again.

"You think this is a lot of takes?" he said when Kaeya complained. "Robert Zemeckis had to film the City Hall clock scene in *Back to the Future* over thirty times. Anyway, I'm almost done. Just let me get a close-up of the computer."

Kaeya was tired and had no idea who Robert Zemeckis was, but she wasn't complaining. Sam was in his zone, and even though her date was in an hour, she was having fun.

Her dad seemed happy too. He watched them film, brought them snacks, even asked if Sam and Thatcher wanted to stay for dinner.

A lot of people would have hated him hovering like that, but not Kaeya. She wanted him there. Her friends were proof that Glen Canyon was working.

"Come on, Sam," complained Thatcher, who was sitting on the armrest of Kaeya's desk chair. "I can't feel my legs anymore."

Sam panned across the keyboard. "Keep typing, but don't say anything," he said.

She obeyed, typing **Robert Zemeckis is holding me hostage** in bold Bookman font.

Thatcher leaned over and typed something himself. Just smile. It'll be over soon.

Kaeya typed back. *I'm getting nervous.*

Thatcher answered. *About Robert Zemeckis?*

No, silly. About LuLu's.

I've barely noticed your tics today. You'll do awesome.

Ya think?

Yeah, really. Don't worry.

Kaeya looked at her watch. It was almost seven. She needed to start getting ready, but she didn't say anything to the guys. Because for some reason, she wanted to stay.

THATCHER

After a few more takes, Sam was done.

"I can drop you off, Thatcher," he said as he reached for his jacket. "It's on my way."

Of course, he wanted Kaeya to drop him off, to listen to her voice and breathe in her perfume again. But she was running late. He should go with Sam.

"Um, yeah, sure," he said.

Kaeya stood quietly at the open front door. "I can still take you, Thatcher," she said.

"N-no, it's fine. You go get ready," he answered.

Kaeya nodded, then reached over and gave Thatcher a hug. The hug wasn't tight, but it hurt, on the inside.

"That's the hug I owe you from last night," she said.

His face was turning red. He could feel it. "Bye," he answered softly.

"See ya, K!" Sam called over his shoulder as he lugged his studio lights down Kaeya's juniper tree-lined driveway.

Thatcher noticed. She hadn't hugged Sam.

It was dark now, and cold. Still reeling from the hug, he put his hands in his pockets and stepped down onto the driveway, where Kaeya's dad was getting something out of the trunk of his car.

"Thanks for letting us come over, Mr. Garay," Thatcher said as he walked by.

Kaeya's dad looked up. He seemed surprised.

"Wait," he called. "Aren't you taking Kaeya to LuLu's?'

I wish, Thatcher thought, realizing Mr. Garay was confusing him with Kieran.

"No, um, I'm Thatcher. Kieran's the one taking her to coffee."

"Oh, I'm sorry. I must be getting old." He laughed as he dipped his head back into the trunk.

Thatcher turned and started toward Sam, who'd already honked his horn once. But before Thatcher reached the end of the driveway, Mr. Garay called him back

"Thatcher. Can I ask you something?" he said."Sure."

"This Kieran, is he an okay guy?"

Thatcher wished he could tell him that Kieran was a creep, a player with a new girlfriend every week, but that would be cruel.

"I haven't really talked to him," he answered. "But Kaeya's pretty smart. I'm sure he's all right."

"Well, you let me know if you dig up any dirt on the guy, okay?" Mr. Garay said with a wink. Was he joking? Probably. Thatcher smiled back.

On the way back, Sam blasted movie sound tracks at full volume. But Thatcher hardly noticed. He was too busy thinking about Kaeya and how beautiful she would look walking into LuLu's.

KAEYA

She ticked a few times as she was getting ready. And on the drive over, she did the new animal sounding thing, twice. But now that she was here, she felt surprisingly okay...except for the nervous stomach.

LuLu's was usually packed with students. But not tonight. It was late, and quiet, too quiet. It would be hard to hide her TS in here.

She spotted Kieran sitting under a Van Gogh print, his army surplus backpack on the empty seat next to him.

"Hey." She smiled as she waved her fingers in his direction.

He smiled back, perfectly. "Hey back," he said.

This is gonna work, she told herself as she gave him a quick hug.

Kieran lifted his backpack and motioned for her to sit. The chair was close to his, really close due to the ant-sized table.

"You look good," he said as she sat down.

"Thanks," she said, thinking he didn't look too bad himself. He was wearing his Manchester City jacket unzipped, with a white V-neck underneath. And he smelled good, like shampoo.

There were two cups on the table, along with a couple of giant chocolate chunk cookies. "I got you a latte and dessert," he said. "It's a down payment for all the calculus help you're going to give me tonight."

Kaeya smiled, took a sip, then angrily placed the cup back on the table.

"Something wrong?" he said.

"You specifically promised me a caramel latte. This is mocha!"

Kieran looked confused. When their eyes locked, Kaeya smiled.

"Oh, you're kidding. Right?"

Humor. It was Kaeya's friend. She'd need lots of it to survive the night.

"That was way too easy." She laughed as she took another sip. "Thanks, by the way. This is good."

In reality, Kaeya hated mocha lattes, but the fact that Kieran had bought it for her made the drink tolerable.

The first few minutes went well. And with the conversation flowing easily from chai tea to striped socks to EDM music, they didn't even open their math books. Eventually, the conversation drifted over to Kieran's game against Troy. Luckily, Kaeya knew soccer. Her parents were from Argentina, a country that had won the World Cup twice.

THATCHER

Thatcher smelled his sweater, the one she'd left her scent on. He could almost feel her fingers on his back from the hug.

Kieran was with her now, drinking coffee, smelling her violets, staring at the faint freckles on her nose. The thought was a knife carving graffiti on his heart. But for some reason, he found himself whispering a silent prayer. It didn't make sense, not at all, but he wanted Kaeya's date to go well.

KAEYA

Kieran was talking about overtime and getting totally into it, when she felt it in her neck. It always started with the neck. She pulled both ends of her scarf down, as if her TS was a cold breeze.

"So it went to penalties, and I was second."

Kaeya's face twitched, but Kieran was too into his story to notice.

"And I didn't put enough bend on it, so it just flew wide."

Another twist. Worse this time. She needed to interrupt, to get her mind off her face.

"Have you seen that movie, the one with the girl who plays soccer and...*Arrr*!" The dreaded animal pirate had arrived. She twisted the squeak into a sneeze, but it was hardly convincing.

"*Bend It like Beckham*," Kieran said as if he hadn't noticed. Had she gotten away with the sneeze fake? She wasn't sure.

"Yeah! I spent hours in my backyard trying to curve my kicks after watching that."

"You ever learn how?" he asked.

Another chorus of *Arrr!*-sneeze combinations. It was time for plan B.

"Hold that thought. I need to go to the restroom," she said.

"Sure," he said. "The less time we have for calculus, the better."

Kaeya fled to the tiny bathroom, shut the door, and let out a loud string of vocalizations. She snapped her rubber bands, hard, then splashed her face with water. She wasn't going down. Not tonight. In a few minutes, she'd be ready for another round of Kieran.

THATCHER

He dropped the sweater on the floor next to his desk and began scribbling a quote on the back of an old math page. The words came easy this time because they were his own, made up because he couldn't think of anything else to post. When he was done, he messed up his hair some more and set up his phone.

As the seconds counted down, he held up his message.

Love means watering her garden with your tears.

And as he waited for the camera to click, a realization fell on him like a gentle rain. Maybe the words meant something. Maybe he was onto something. Maybe love, real love, was more than unicorns and rainbows. Maybe it meant hanging on even when it tore you apart.

KAEYA

She'd flicked rubber bands, coughed like she had pneumonia, and teared up behind bathroom stall doors...but she was surviving. Barely.

Was she enjoying herself? She wasn't sure. But the plan was to stick this out until the end. And the plan was all that mattered.

On her third trip back from the bathroom, Kieran held up her cell phone.

"You got a text," he said as he stared down at the screen. Kaeya reached out for the phone, but Kieran pulled it away. "Whoa, your inbox is almost full! You know you can delete them all at once."

"NO!" she yelled as she grabbed Kieran's arm. Her tone was too harsh, and she tried to think of something cute to save the situation. But she couldn't, because he'd almost erased her texts, and she didn't know what she'd do without them.

"I d-didn't read your texts. Promise," he stammered as he handed the phone back.

"No, it's not that!" she explained. "It's just that there are texts from my mom in there...from a long time ago. They're like my security blanket. I read them when

I'm stressed."

Kieran put his hand on hers and held it there. "I'm totally sorry. I had no idea that—"

"No worries," interrupted Kaeya. "You didn't know." His hand felt warm. She blushed, and he slid it away.

"It's getting late, and I haven't even helped you with your calculus yet," she blurted.

"That's okay," he said. "This wasn't really about the math."

Kaeya's pulse quickened. Was this his way of saying that he liked her? Everything was escalating so quickly. Incredible.

More small talk, a couple more sips of coffee, and her body had had enough. She stood, grabbed her purse, and reached over the table for a quick hug. But before she could say good-bye, Kieran interrupted.

"So...you going to Lanterns?" he asked.

She couldn't believe what she was hearing. "No.

I'm pretty new here, so it's not like I know a lot of people."

"Okay," he said as he stood and held up her jacket.

Okay? Was that all he was going to say?

She slid into her jacket, and they hugged. And that was it. For now.

But on the way home, she analyzed the situation, deeply. And by the time she pulled into her driveway, utterly exhausted, she'd come to a conclusion. Kieran's *longer than a friend would* hug and his question about the dance meant something.

He was going to ask her to Lanterns. She was sure of it.

14

SATURDAY

THATCHER

Kaeya's car was nowhere to be seen. Had Sam even called her?

"You said 9:30, right?" Thatcher asked as he stepped up onto Sam's front porch. He didn't mention Kaeya. That would be too obvious.

"Yeah, that'll give us enough time to shoot the scene where they leave to the airport, and maybe get some shots inside."

Thatcher looked back toward the driveway. Still empty.

"Don't worry. She's coming," Sam said as he wiped the lens of his camera.

"Cool."

Sam put his camera down. "You should ask her, you know."

"Ask her?"

"To Lanterns," he answered, as if it were the most obvious question in the world. "She's so set on going with that Kieran guy that she's not seeing it."

Thatcher looked at his feet. "Seeing what?"

"Oh, come on. It's like *You've Got Mail*, or *While You Were Sleeping*, or every romantic comedy in the history of nineties-era romantic comedies. They always start with some girl in a relationship with the wrong guy. It's not like the dude is bad or anything. He's just not the soul mate she's been looking for."

He set the camera down and stared out at the driveway. "But the one she's *supposed* to fall in love with, the misfit plumber who paints or something, is always sitting right under her nose."

"So I'm like the misfit plumber?"

"No, you're more of a Sam Baldwin type," Sam answered.

Thatcher shook his head and laughed. "Sam who?" he asked.

"Dude. Sam Baldwin. From *Sleepless in Seattle*. The movie that defined the nineties-era romcom genre. Don't tell me you haven't seen it.*"

"Um...doesn't ring a bell."

"Dude! You *have* to watch it. Promise me you'll watch it!" he urged.

His intensity was amusing, and Thatcher couldn't help but smile. He was about to promise that he would, when he noticed a car pulling up, Kaeya's.

Sam stood. "She's into you, Thatcher. I can tell. She just doesn't know it yet."

Thatcher wanted to believe him. But Sam knew movies, not love. He'd probably never had a girlfriend in his life.

Kaeya was walking up the driveway now. He adored the way she walked, like she was on a mission to save the planet.

She stepped onto the porch and hugged him. First. And he hoped beyond hope that Sam was right.

KAEYA

Kaeya spun circles on Sam's office chair. "This is actually going to happen." She knew she beamed as she set her can of Coke down on an action figure–cluttered desk.

Sam had been in the kitchen for at least ten minutes, discussing something in Korean with his grandma and mom. But she didn't mind. Thatcher seemed to open up more when they were alone.

"I mean, why would he mention Lanterns if he wasn't going to ask? Right?"

"Right," answered Thatcher, who was leaning against a *Jurassic Park* poster. His tone was distant. She wondered why.

"You hesitated," she said as she spun in his direction.

"Relax, Kaeya. He's gonna ask. You're like this perfect person. Why wouldn't he?" He was blushing, for some reason. She thought that was cute.

The morning had been fun, a disorganized mess, but still fun. It was weird though. Even though they'd pretty much botched every line, Sam didn't even seem to care. It was like he was oblivious to the disaster they were making of his script.

Eventually, Sam came back. He looked depressed. "Look, guys. I've got to go pick up my dad at the airport," he said. "He's flying in from Korea. My sister was supposed to pick him up, but she has to take care of my little nephew."

Thatcher stood and stretched. "That's okay. We can film the final scene on Monday."

"Have you even written a final scene?" asked Kaeya. "I didn't see it in your script."

"Not yet. I'll finish it this weekend. You guys don't mind kissing, do you?"

Now she was the one blushing.

"Sam! No way," Thatcher argued. "Of course she doesn't want to kiss me."

He was trying to save her, and she appreciated it. But he didn't have to. "Hey, what's a romantic movie without a kiss?"

"Awesome!" said Sam. "I'll e-mail you the scene when I'm done."

She glanced at Thatcher as they walked outside, and wondered what it would be like.

THATCHER

They walked to her car together, then waved as Sam backed out of the driveway. It was time to go, but his feet weren't cooperating.

"Wanna see my dream dress?" she asked.

There it was again, Lanterns. She'd talked about it all morning long.

Kaeya held up her phone. Thatcher moved close.

"Youtopia. Way out of my price range," she said as she zoomed in. "They have a store at South Coast Plaza."

The white dress was creative and fresh. Definitely Kaeya...but she was buying it for Kieran.

"Cool," he said, an antonym of his actual feelings.

"I'm definitely wearing my brown leather boots. There's no way I'm wearing high heels out at the lake."

Thatcher crossed his arms and stared at the asphalt. "Yeah...that would probably be a good idea." He looked at his watch, as if time really mattered. "Well, I better go," he said as he began to walk away.

But she grabbed his wrist and actually held on for a couple of seconds. "I'm going to some vintage dress shops today...to find one that's cheaper," she said. "Wanna come?"

She might as well have asked, *Wanna come watch me gather the wood and gasoline I'm gonna use to burn up your dreams?*

He was about to say no. It would have been less painful. But he couldn't help it. She was a tractor beam that pulled him in like an atomic vacuum cleaner. "Sure," he answered reluctantly.

"Yay! I'll buy you lunch," she said. "Let's meet in front of the Empire Theater."

Thatcher knew the place. Everyone did. It was in the heart of old-town Corona, an artsy enclave of vintage clothes stores and antique shops.

As he watched her get in her car and drive away, he wondered. Why was he torturing himself like this?

KAEYA

They shared a pizza in the grassy center of the roundabout, by the fountain. And as the cars spun round, they talked.

She told him how she wished that the lanterns still flew, like in *Tangled*. And he mentioned he liked T. S. Eliot's poetry—because of lines like *April is the cruelest month* and *This is the way the world ends*. Kaeya, who'd never heard of T. S. Eliot, was intrigued.

She held her green jacket closed. It was getting cold. "'Love means watering her garden with your tears,'" she said randomly.

"You saw my quote!" said Thatcher. He seemed surprised.

"Yeah, and apparently a lot of other people did too."

"I guess. There were like nine hundred views this morning."

"It's pretty. Where'd you find it?"

Thatcher looked embarrassed and proud at the same time. "I wrote it myself," he said.

"No way," she said. "What does it mean?"

"I don't know. I just liked the sound of it," he said.

"What about 'Love is a cold night, warmed by the voice of a friend?' Did you write that one too?"

There he was, blushing again. Kaeya couldn't help but smile.

THATCHER

The blue dress looked perfect on Kaeya, and he told her so. But apparently it wasn't perfect enough.

"It's too short," she said as she twirled in front of the mirror. They'd been in the trendy little store for at least twenty minutes, and she still hadn't found a dress she liked.

Kaeya yelled something as she popped back into the dressing room. It almost sounded like a bark. She'd been making the sound all afternoon. Thatcher didn't mind, but a couple of the other customers did. He could see their blatantly annoyed looks. Didn't they realize that she couldn't help it?

"Hey, I've been talking about Lanterns all day," she said as she changed. "I'm starting to feel like a narcissist. How have things been going for you? You know, with your family?"

"The same. Dad still a jerk. Mom still waiting for him to come back," he said. The words sounded bitter, too bitter. He needed to add a little more happy to his tone.

"Have you even talked to him, you know, about how you're feeling?"

"Um, yeah, that's not gonna happen. We'd just end up in a fight."

Kaeya came out of the stall with the dress folded over her arm. She placed it on a rack and let out another bark. He pretended not to notice.

"Just finish with I love you, and you can say anything," she said.

"What?" he asked.

"*I love yous*. They have a way of disarming people."

"I'll have to try that the next time I get in a fight with Quentin," he joked as he watched her rummage through another clearance rack.

Kaeya laughed. "You suck! I love you."

"Or, shut up. I love you," called Thatcher.

"See, don't you feel better now?" She smiled.

Suddenly, her eyes lit up. She'd found something. "Ooh, how about this?" she said as she held up a 1940s-style polka-dotted dress. It looked like something out of *I Love Lucy*.

Thatcher was about to tell her that it would look cute on her, but he was interrupted.

"Excuse me, miss," said a stern-looking middle-aged woman. Her name tag said she was the store's manager.

"Yes?" answered Kaeya politely.

"Your behavior is disturbing some of the customers," she lectured. "You need to either keep it down or leave."

Kaeya turned red. "I'm sorry. I can't help it. I have Tourette's," she explained. Thatcher was surprised at how polite Kaeya was being. The woman was a total jerk, and he felt like telling her off.

The woman walked away, and Kaeya put the dress back on the rack. They continued shopping for a few minutes, but it wasn't the same. Kaeya seemed subdued, like the wind had been knocked out of her. And when she barked again, she looked mortified.

KAEYA

"Miss, I'm going to have to ask you to leave." The manager scowled.

People were staring now, openly. Kaeya placed the dress she was holding on top of a rack and hurried toward the door.

"I can ring that up for you before you leave, if you want," said the manager. She was cheery again, as if the entire awkward scene had never happened.

When she and Thatcher got to the sidewalk, Thatcher suddenly barged back in. Kaeya followed but stayed close to the door.

"Oh, so she's not good enough for your store, but you'll still take her money?" he said.

"I was simply trying to be polite, sir," said the manager in a condescending tone.

"And were you also being polite when you humiliated her?"

Thatcher, who was usually so mild, seemed furious, and Kaeya worried that he was going to lose it like he did at school. "Let's just go," she said as she grabbed his hand and tried pulling him to the door. But he wasn't going anywhere.

The manager seemed offended, as if she were the one who had just been treated like garbage. "Sir, please lower your voice. You're disturbing the customers."

Thatcher was about to say something, but Kaeya squeezed his hand. "She's not worth it," she begged as she pulled him outside.

As they walked down the sidewalk, Thatcher was still mad. She could tell by the intensity of his steps. But out here, she appreciated his frustration. Except for her father, no one had ever stood up for her like that.

"I'm sorry," Thatcher mumbled when they reached her car. He was standing close, so close she could count his long eyelashes.

"Don't be," she told him. "The only reason I stopped you was because I didn't want you to get in trouble. I mean, you don't want a repeat of the Quentin disaster, do you?"

"I don't know," he said with a shrug. "Maybe I do."

At first, Kaeya didn't know what he meant, but then she looked down and realized...

She was still holding his hand.

THATCHER

He remembered the words from one of Scout's picture books, the words he'd scribbled on the inside cover of his journal. As of that afternoon, they were his favorite words in the world.

Pel the Panda sat next to Pearl on the old brick wall.

"Pearl," he whispered softly.

"Yes, Pel?" the pig answered, her voice full of friendship.

"When we're together, the day makes sense," said Pel as he reached for her paw.

"Silly bear, of course it does." She laughed. "Love always makes sense."

KAEYA

Kaeya gazed at the glowing stars on her ceiling. Her mom had put them there when Kaeya was in third grade so she could make wishes anytime she wanted. But tonight she had no idea what to wish for, because she'd held Thatcher's hand, and it was warm and soft...and confusing.

Reaching up toward Polaris, she traced down to the Big Dipper. An hour earlier, Kieran had called, asking obvious questions about her favorite restaurant and what kind of flowers she liked. Definitely the planning stages of a Lanterns ask, the moment she'd dreamed of for weeks. So why was she feeling so empty?

THATCHER

The Martha Baines T-shirt would be the same, but not the hair. Tonight he needed to look perfect, for Kaeya, who'd held his hand for at least five minutes, her fingers intertwined with his so that they formed one shape, a perfect shape he'd remember forever.

Looking into the mirror, he remembered Sam's words: *She likes you. She just doesn't know it.* Just that morning, the words had sounded insane, but here in the afterglow of the afternoon they seemed almost rational.

And that was what hurt the most, being close but a million miles away.

Blake, and Wordsworth, and every other romantic poetic stuck in Thatcher's head sang their opinions. But Amélie Sarchet sang the loudest: *Take a risk, Thatcher, or else you'll never know!* But what did she know? She was a French romantic, far too emotional to understand the intricacies of twenty-first-century love.

And then again, unlike Sam, she knew love, had written beautifully about it for decades, understood it like no one else.

He read Sarchet's words for the millionth time, then copied them down:

> *There comes a time when the fear of being alone*
> *outweighs the fear of rejection*
> *And in this glorious imbalance,*
> *Love is born.*

Sarchet was right. He was afraid. Of doing nothing and losing everything. Of living life without Kaeya. Of watching her fall in love with someone else.

So he leaned his phone against a stack of books, held up the quote, and stepped back. No one would know what the message meant. But so what? It was a personal message, his battle cry, his flying ninja kick into the door of the unknown.

Tomorrow he'd ask Kaeya to Lanterns...before Kieran did.

KAEYA

Kaeya turned toward the window and watched as a tree branch played drums on the pane. Had Thatcher posted another meme? She picked up her phone. He had.

> *There comes a time when the fear of being alone*
> *outweighs the fear of rejection*
> *And in this glorious imbalance,*
> *Love is born.*
> *—Amélie Sarchet*

She twirled the quote in her head, like a loose bracelet. The words made her nervous. Because they had something to do with her. Because he'd blushed when she came out of the dressing room in the light-blue dress. Because she liked the fact that he did. Because she'd held his hand for way too long.

A sick feeling made its way down to her stomach. Had she been leading him on? Had she been using his shoulder to cry on because there was no one else around?

She sat up in bed, heart racing. She *had* led him on. She was a horrible person, absolutely horrible. It was time to pull away. Or maybe not. She wasn't sure...

Because his hand fit perfectly in hers, as if it were the missing piece of a puzzle.

15

SUNDAY

THATCHER

"So when are you gonna do it?" asked Sam, his voice Sunday-morning groggy on the other end of the line.

"Right after your last scene, when we kiss," answered Thatcher.

Sure, it wasn't a spectacular Lanterns ask, but it would definitely be a surprise, and hopefully a good one.

"Awesome!" said Sam. "Just like in that movie *Summer in September*!"

Sam was breaking up, so Thatcher moved outside for a better connection.

"Dude, I have the perfect setting for you," Sam continued.

"Forget the setting. I just need to ask her before Kieran does."

"But setting is everything. What if *The African Queen* had been filmed in Fresno? Or *Casablanca* in Las Vegas?"

"Okay, okay, I get it. What were you thinking?"

"Paradigm Studios," Sam said after a long pause. "They have this European-looking back lot. Totally looks like Prague."

"You're kidding, right?" said Thatcher.

"I'm dead serious. I have a coupon for the studio tour."

"You have a coupon? Sam, I've been on that tour. They're not gonna let us hop off the tram wherever we want."

"Who says we need permission?"

"So you want us *sneak* onto the back lot? That's insane."

"Not insane, incredible, and easy. I've been on the tour a zillion times."

"Um yeah, like there won't be any security guards at a major film studio."

"Well, of course there's security. But there's this part towards the end of the tour where you get off at this sound stage to watch a special-effects demonstration. The European back lot is right behind it."

Thatcher shook his head. He wasn't buying it. Not at all.

"All we have to do is walk into the theater and out the emergency exit. The show is twenty-three minutes long. I've timed it. We'll film the scene and sneak back before it ends."

"Look, Sam, I'm in the middle of a suspension right now, and I can't afford getting into any more trouble. Maybe we can film the scene at my house."

"Your house? Thatcher, come on. You know your street looks nothing like Europe. It would totally ruin the effect."

Sam's plan was insane, stupidly insane, like *skateboarding down the rails of an escalator* insane. But then he went on and on about it being impossible to get caught. About how if they did get caught, nothing would happen. About how perfect it would be for the both of them. He'd spent years daydreaming up all the details, and Thatcher could feel his resistance cracking.

"Thatcher, we need to do this. Today. Before you change your mind. Please?"

Sam was begging now, as if it were a dying wish, and Thatcher almost felt bad for him. He ran his fingers through his hair. "We're gonna get caught."

"It's totally dark in the sound stage. No one will see us leave."

"But you can't guarantee that."

"Look, I'm 99.9 percent sure we won't get caught. Just trust me. I know what I'm doing."

He closed his eyes and sighed. Sam's idea was ridiculous. But the back lot of a major film studio for his Lanterns ask? That would be pretty awesome.

"All right," he agreed. "But only if we can convince Kaeya."

"We don't have to convince her," said Sam, "at least not until we get there."

They talked for a few more minutes, with Thatcher shaking his head in agony, and Sam practically screaming with excitement. The plan was crazy...and somehow romantic, crazy romantic.

KAEYA

"Where've you been all morning?" said Sam. He sounded exasperated.

She put down the box of Cheerios she was about to pour. "Is something wrong?" she asked.

"We have a movie trailer to finish. Remember?" he said.

"Oh yeah, that's right," she said, smiling at the intensity in his tone.

"So what are you doing?" he asked.

"Um, eating a bowl of cereal?"

"I mean, this afternoon. Can you shoot today?"

Kaeya's heart raced. The kiss. She was available, but did she want to be?

"Thatcher and I were thinking of filming at Paradigm," Sam continued. "I have this BOGO coupon for the tour. You won't even have to pay."

Kaeya pulled her hair in mock agony. "Look, I'm not sure if I..."

"Yeah, they have this European back lot, and it's perfect for the final scene," he went on, as if she wasn't even on the line.

She'd never been on the Paradigm tour before, but of course she'd heard of it. "So do they allow just anyone to film there?"

"Oh, it'll be all right. We can shoot the scene really quick. No big deal," he said, making it sound as if it were the easiest thing in the world.

She sat back in her chair and stared at the ceiling. Kissing Thatcher *was* a big deal. And filming the kiss while a bunch of tourists stared at them wouldn't make things any easier.

But if they finished filming today, it would be over with. And then she'd have the rest of the week to focus on Kieran, and Lanterns, and everything she'd dreamed of.

"When and how?" she asked.

"Pick you up in twenty minutes. Thatcher's driving."

Kaeya cringed. What was she getting herself into? "Ahhh, all right," she said.

"You're to die for Georgette!" Sam screamed, stealing the line from an old Humphrey Bogart movie they'd talked about once.

She hung up and screamed into the empty kitchen. "Kaeya Garay, you are insane!"

THATCHER

The tram lurched around another corner, causing Thatcher to slide into Kaeya. She didn't smile. Not a good sign.

He felt for the note in his pocket, the exact words he'd use to ask her. He'd written them down the night before and practiced them all morning. He was ready. Was she? Judging by the irritated look on her face, probably not.

Sam nudged Thatcher for the millionth time. "Look! See that town square? That's where they filmed the mother ship landing in *The Third Extraction*. Jonathan Kane wanted the actors to look genuinely startled in that scene, so he surprised them by firing a cannon off the roof."

Thatcher nodded. On any other day, he would have loved hearing all of Sam's movie anecdotes. But not today. He was way too nervous. In about five minutes, they'd be hopping off the tram, and his introduction into the world of trespassing would begin.

Kaeya stared vacantly as she sat by the open edge of the tram. She'd been covering her mouth with her sweatshirt the entire ride, probably because of her vocalizations. *Stress*, he thought.

She'd gotten upset when they told her they'd be sneaking onto the back lot, but amazingly, she'd agreed to go along with the plan, which totally surprised him. It was almost as if she was dying to get it over with, like a tooth extraction or something. Which made him doubt the whole *Kaeya is crushing on Thatcher too* theory. Had he misread the signs? Maybe. Or maybe not. He wasn't sure of anything now.

"You okay?" he asked as the tram rolled past a row of massive cement sound stages.

"'What does okay even mean? Is it some lame excuse for failure? I want better than okay. I want perfect.'" She was quoting lines from Sam's final scene, and she was smiling. Relief.

"'Let me show you what perfect feels like,'" Thatcher said, making kissing sounds.

Kaeya laughed. "That line is so dumb." She whispered so Sam wouldn't hear.

"I know. Right?" he answered. "I think it's all those romantic comedies he watches. They're affecting his judgment."

The tour guide explained how a huge water tank was used to film the underwater scenes in *The Dark Below*, while Sam took pictures.

"Are you okay with this?" she said when the guide had finished.

"I guess. I mean, what's the worst that can happen? They kick us out of the park?"

"No, I mean, are you okay with, you know, kissing me?"

Thatcher looked out at the lot. A group of construction workers were lifting a sign onto the back of a semitruck while a serious-looking woman looked on.

"Yeah, I'm okay with it. Who wouldn't be?" he said. His voice trailed off as he realized what he'd just done. It was out in the open now. He liked her.

The tram stopped before she had a chance to respond. They'd arrived at the sound stage, and the thirty or so passengers were disembarking like excited ants. It was showtime.

KAEYA

Sam raced through the theater like an Olympic speed walker. Luckily, the tour guide was still at the entrance, or she would have gotten suspicious.

"Wait up!" Kaeya whispered as she followed him across a row of empty seats.

When he reached the other side, he pushed through a long, dark curtain and disappeared. This was it. She took a step forward, then froze. No way. She wasn't going through with this.

"Come on. It's fine," whispered Thatcher as he grabbed her hand and nudged her from behind. His hand felt good, too good, and she wondered if she should let go. But she was scared, and she needed this, so she held on tighter and dove into the abyss.

The hall on the other side of the curtain was narrow and full of lighting equipment. She could tell that all this sneaking around was getting to Sam. He seemed pale and out of breath as he waited by the double doors.

"Sam, you don't look so good," said Thatcher. "Are you sure you want to go through with this?"

Sam stood straight and smiled. "'Life's not about the amount of breaths you take, but the moments that take your breath away,'" he said as he pushed through the door. "Will Smith, *Hitch*," he whispered over his shoulder as he jogged onto the lot.

Kaeya squinted into the sun. They'd done it. They were actually on the Paradigm back lot. And as far as

Kaeya could tell, no one had followed them. Good. In a matter of minutes, the scene would be filmed, the kiss would be over, and she could finally get back to her own movie...the movie that starred Kieran.

THATCHER

The back lot was huge and creative and incredible, with rows and rows of fake buildings built to look like New York, Tokyo, and London. The street they were currently on looked more like 1920s Chicago than Europe though, and Thatcher was starting to wonder whether Sam had gotten them lost.

"I thought you said the European back lot was behind the special-effects Stage?" he asked as they turned onto another empty street.

"It *was*, on the map," said Sam. He seemed confused, which made Thatcher nervous.

"Wait, I thought you said you've done this a zillion times," said Thatcher, checking his watch.

"No, I said I've gone *on the tour* a zillion times. But I've dreamed of sneaking onto the lot for years though, if that makes you feel any better."

"Oh great," Thatcher said. "Now we're going to..."

"Guys, our tram is gonna leave in like ten minutes," interrupted Kaeya. "Let's just film the scene now and get out of here."

"I guess this can pass as Prague," Sam conceded as he fiddled with his camera. "Just start walking down the sidewalk, and I'll follow. Then stop in front of that café over there, say your lines, and kiss."

Thatcher's hands were starting to shake from stress, so he put them in his pockets. He was about to kiss her, and more importantly, he was about to ask her to Lanterns. He went over the lines in his head, the ones for Sam's movie and the ones for his ask.

Sam gave the signal, and they started to walk. "Are you okay?" he said dramatically as they strolled past a poster-plastered brick wall.

"What does okay even mean? I want better than okay. I want perfect," she answered with Sam's camera inches from her face.

They reached their mark, and Thatcher stopped. They turned to face each other. "Let me show you what perfect feels like," he said. He leaned in to kiss her, but Kaeya jerked away.

"HA HA!" she yelled as he let her go. "I'm so sorry," she said.

She was stressed. Thatcher wondered whether they should just give up and go back. "No worries, Kaeya," he said as he watched her face twist into a scowl.

"Quiet," whispered Sam as he pulled his camera down.

"Are you kidding me? She can't help it," said Thatcher.

"Shhh!" said Sam. "Someone's coming."

Sam pointed toward the end of the long street, where a golf cart was moving down a small hill. The cart was still far away, but traveling in their direction. Thatcher froze. "It's a security guard," he said.

Kaeya turned toward Thatcher. "Do you think he saw us?" she asked.

"I don't know, but let's get out of here," he answered.

Thatcher led the way, walking in the opposite direction as if nothing was wrong. "Just act natural," he said as Kaeya and Sam followed.

The guard was still about a couple of blocks away when they reached the corner. Thatcher had no idea which way to go, so he guessed left. Then once out of the guard's view, they ran in the general direction of the sound stages. They were almost there, when Sam slowed to a stop.

Kaeya ran back to him. "What's wrong?" she asked, putting her hand on his back. He was struggling for breath.

"Just a cramp," he said. "Give me a minute."

But they didn't have a minute. Thatcher could hear the electric whirr of the golf cart's engine. In a matter of seconds, it would turn the corner, and they'd be history.

KAEYA

Kaeya scanned the buildings for a place to hide. *Café.*
Boulangerie. Boucher. Apparently, they'd reached the
Paris section of the back lot. "Over there," she cried,
pointing toward the open double doors of an old French
movie theater.

Thatcher and Sam needed little convincing. They
followed her across the street and piled through the
cinema doors behind her.

The building's interior was more garage than
movie theater, with plywood walls and barren cement
floors. "They're just shells," explained Sam, who
could hardly speak because of his wheezing. "The real
interior shots are filmed on a sound stage."

At that particular moment, she couldn't care less
about the logistics of moviemaking. They'd already
missed the tram back to the studio entrance and had no
way of getting back.She looked over at Sam, who was
gasping for air. Scary.

"You're probably just having a panic attack," said
Thatcher as he kneeled down in front of him. "Breathe
slowly."

"It's all right," he answered. "Happens all the
time."

"Do you have an inhaler?" Kaeya asked as she
joined them on the cold floor. She'd seen him use one in
class before.

"No. It's not asthma. It's my heart," he explained,
waving them off. "Long story."

She looked at Thatcher with raised eyebrows. His heart? Why hadn't he mentioned this before?

Thatcher shrugged.

The cart was close now, its engines growing louder as it passed. Kaeya held her breath until, eventually, the sound faded. Were they in the clear? She hoped so.

A couple of minutes passed. Nothing. She reached for Thatcher's hand, and he helped her to her feet. "Do you think he's gone?" she whispered.

Letting go of her hand, he tiptoed toward the open door. Kaeya followed. He leaned against the wall, listened, then raised a finger to his lips. There were footsteps moving in their direction.

Kaeya pressed herself against Thatcher's back. They were trespassers, and the security guard was only feet away. They needed to be completely silent, but her brain wasn't cooperating. She snapped the rubber bands on her wrist, bounced up and down on her heels, and pulled her hair, but there was no choice. "HA HA HA!" she yelled into the air.

More footsteps. An intimidating figure at the door. It was over.

Thatcher

The expressionless security guard was gone. He'd dumped them off at some administration building, taken their information, then left. And for the last ten minutes, they'd been alone in a depressingly barren office, waiting for him to return.

Thatcher was stressed. First the fight with Quentin, now this. What would Mom say? Mostly though, he was worried about Kaeya. Her tics were worse than ever. Too much stress. "My dad's gonna kill me," she whispered as she rocked back and forth on the plastic folding chair. The air-conditioned room was freezing, and she was shivering.

Thatcher blamed himself. "They'll probably just kick us out of the park and tell us not to come back," he said in a feeble attempt to make her feel better. From the way she buried herself in the hood of her sweatshirt, it wasn't working.

Sam, on the other hand, looked thrilled. He watched in awe as a well-dressed studio staff person walked past the open door. "I can't believe actually I'm here," he said. "Tim Stafford, Sean Martin, all the great producers have had offices in this building." He'd been talking nonstop since they'd arrived, and Thatcher was getting annoyed.

"Sam, just be quiet," begged Kaeya. Her voice was sweet, even when she was annoyed, another thing to love.

A group of office workers walked by, followed by a hip-looking girl in black. She held a journal and was talking to a slightly overweight, bearded guy. The guy looked like he was in his forties.

"No stinkin' way," Sam said as he got out of his chair and raced to the hall. "Mr. Owens!" he yelled. "I'm a huge fan of your work."

The man, taken aback at Sam's surprise attack, was nice enough to smile. "Well, thanks." He laughed as he shook Sam's hand. "People usually don't recognize me."

"They should!" gushed Sam. "You're the most creative screenwriter in the industry. I mean, *My Forever* blew my mind."

"Oh, you're way too kind," said the bearded guy, who actually seemed flattered. He poked his head into the room and nodded to Thatcher and Kaeya. Thatcher waved.

The woman, who must have been his assistant, looked at her watch as if to signal that they didn't have time for overzealous fans. But Bearded Guy ignored her. "So what brings you guys to Paradigm?" he asked.

Thatcher explained their predicament, purposely describing in extra detail Sam's lifelong dream of filming on the Paradigm back lot.

The screenwriter laughed. "So you're guerilla filmmakers," he said. "Congratulations on getting past security...sort of."

There was a commotion at the door, and Bearded Guy stepped aside. The security guard was back, this time with a stern-looking woman. It was the suspension meeting all over again, and Thatcher felt sick.

"As you're minors, we've decided to let your parents handle this," said the woman as she paced in without an introduction. She picked up a phone and began to dial. Kaeya looked mortified.

Bearded Guy put his hand on the phone. "Wait a second. Don't you think you're being a little harsh?" he said.

"Harsh?" said the woman. "They were trespassing, which is a misdemeanor, I might add. They're getting off easy."

"Come on. They're just kids. It's not like they were painting graffiti on the sets or anything."

"You don't know what they were planning to do," argued the woman.

Bearded Guy turned toward Thatcher. "Would you guys mind stepping outside for second?" he said.

Thatcher hesitated. Would that be okay with Scary Security Lady? She didn't say anything, so he assumed it was. The stepped into the hall, and the door closed behind them.

After nearly ten minutes, Bearded Guy emerged with a huge smile on his face. "You're off the hook," he whispered. "Now get out of here before the Wicked Witch of the West changes her mind. My assistant, Ms. Wyatt, will show you to the front gate."

Sam tackled the stranger with a hug. "Thanks *so* much, Mr. Owens!" he said.

"No worries." The screenwriter laughed. "Just remember to thank me when you win your first Academy Award."

In a matter of minutes, they were back in the parking lot. "That was awesome!" laughed Sam as he danced through parked cars. Thatcher had never seen him so hyper before.

"You guys owe me, *big time*," Kaeya lectured as she punched Thatcher on the shoulder.

"Hey, we didn't *force* you to come," he argued, walking backward to face her.

"No, you tricked me into coming because you guys are manipulators. That's what you are!" she yelled.

Startled by this schizophrenic change of tone, Thatcher froze...and that was when Kaeya smiled.

"And I love you," she finished.

"Don't scare me like that!" he said as he tossed his empty water bottle at her. "I thought you were serious."

"See, I told you. Add an *I love you* at the end, and you can say anything you want."

"You're mean."

"No, I'm extraordinarily witty."

"No, you're an idiot," he quipped. "And I love you back."

KAEYA

They were stuck in LA traffic, but they were free, and that was all that mattered.

"They didn't even check my camera," said Sam incredulously. "I thought for sure they were going to make me delete my footage."

"What footage?" said Thatcher. "We barely got five feet before the security guard showed up."

"Still, best day ever," said Sam as he stared out at the downtown skyscrapers.

"You mean *worst* day ever," said Kaeya.

"Are you kidding me?" argued Sam. "Not even close."

Thatcher drove quietly. He hadn't said much since leaving. She nudged him. "You're the tiebreaker, Thatcher. Best or worst day ever?"

"Well, I wouldn't say it was my *best* day ever, but it definitely wasn't my worst," he said with a smile.

She slapped Thatcher's arm. "You're so indecisive."

"Ouch," he said.

"Kaeya, you're delusional if you think this is a *worst day ever*," chimed Sam from the backseat. "I bet you've never had a *worst day ever* in your life...and I love you."

There was a stalled car up ahead, blocking one of the lanes.

"By the way, take that as a compliment," he added as Thatcher eased into the next lane. "I mean, look at you. Everyone loves you. You look perfect, act perfect, are perfect. You have no idea what commoners like Thatcher and I have to put up with."

Kaeya turned around. "Okay, I challenge you, Sam. *Worst day ever*. We tell our worst days ever to Mr. Indecisive here, and he picks the most pitiful. Loser buys candy for the winner."

"Hey, no name calling!" quipped Thatcher as the car inched forward.

"Challenge accepted," chimed Sam as he popped his head between the two front seats. "I get to start though."

Kaeya turned off the radio and crossed her arms. "Fire away."

"So when I was in second grade, my mom bought me this puppy for my eighth birthday," he began. "It was a corgi German shepherd mix. I named him Miso, which means *smile* in Korean. I didn't have a lot of friends back then, so Miso and I were really close. He'd follow me around all day and be waiting on our apartment's balcony when I came home from school."

Kaeya squirmed in her seat. Sam was playing the puppy card, nearly impossible to beat.

"Anyway, when my parents told me we were moving to America, they said I could take him. But then on the day before we were supposed to leave, my dad said we had to leave him behind with our neighbor, something about immigration rules. When we left to the airport, I turned around and saw him waiting for me on the balcony, with his little puppy eyes, completely unaware of the fact that I was never coming back."

"Oh my gosh, Sam! That's *so* sad!" she gasped as she gave Sam's hand a squeeze.

"Yeah, you might as well give up right now," said Thatcher as he turned up the heater. It was getting cold.

"No way," she answered. "I'm not letting a puppy beat me!"

Kaeya sat crisscross on the passenger seat. She was ready.

"So...the Sunday after my mom died, I'm sitting in church—crying because I'm still pretty shaken up—and I feel a tap on my shoulder. I turn around, and this lady's standing there. She was a volunteer usher or something. I didn't recognize her. Anyway, she tells me I can't sit in the main auditorium anymore because I'm disturbing people.

"My dad's furious and wants to leave...but I don't want to, because home reminds me too much of Mom. So he goes out to the car, while I go to this room in the back for crying babies. While I'm sitting there, all alone, with all these parents staring at my tics, and toddlers running to their mommies like I'm a monster, I feel this complete despair, this total emptiness ...like even God is turning His back on me because of my TS."

Complete silence followed, and Thatcher turned to look into her aching eyes.

"Um, nice try, Kaeya...but the puppy wins," he said.

"Yes!" Sam yelled as he punched the roof. "I'll take a pack of Red Vines please."

"Thatcher! You're supposed to be on my side!" she said.

"Nice try. But the whole *God turning His face* thing was a tad bit overdramatic," he explained.

"Well, of course, but I *reeeally* wanted that candy." She fake cried.

Thatcher laughed. They all did. And it felt good.

When the conversation subsided into a peaceful lull, Kaeya sank into her sweatshirt and leaned against the window. Outside, a thousand headlights painted the night like tiny diamonds. They were beautiful.

"You've figured me out, Thatcher," she admitted. "Now I can't mess with you anymore."

Thatcher nodded, as if to say *I know*.

THATCHER

Thatcher ditched the Martha shirt for his newest sweater, a baggy blue one that he wore over a white T-shirt. He made sure his hair was perfect. It needed to be. Because tomorrow morning he'd be asking her to Lanterns.

Grabbing his keys off the dresser, he got back in his car and drove towards the Towers, the hundred year old block of apartments on 14th street. The cool looking buildings faced each other, creating a sort of courtyard with a fountain in the middle. The white washed cement would make for a perfect picture.

The idea wasn't new. He'd been thinking about it for a while. It involved a fire escape, a box of chalk, and Sam, who was waiting for him at the curb. It was late, but there was enough light from the apartments' park like lamps to light the scene like Las Vegas.

"What do you think?" Sam asked, as he pointed down at the oversized bouquet of flowers he'd drawn on the cement. There were yellows, pinks, and purples. Way better than Thatcher could've drawn.

After a quick fist bump, Thatcher got down on his knees and began scribbling the night's quote in huge letters. He felt a bit like a vandal, but he reminded himself that the building's artistic minded residents wouldn't mind. Besides, he was writing in chalk.

When the masterpiece was finished, Sam climbed up the fire escape while Thatcher laid down on the cement. With his legs bent to the left and his right arm outstretched, he looked like he was flying towards the out of reach bouquet.

"You ready?" Sam called from the second floor.

"Fire away," he yelled as he looked up into the camera with the quote, drawn in a comic book looking thought bubble, inches from his head.

When friendship reaches a certain height,
One has no choice but to release the brakes
And race down, wide eyed, towards love
—Jasmine Bean

KAEYA

His meme was there when she checked. At the top of the page where the trending posts were. With over thirty thousand views, his latest meme was going viral. Crazy!

She clicked on the picture to make it bigger and instantly noticed. This wasn't *Marry Me Martha* anymore. This was something bigger. Though Thatcher's eyes looked insecure, he was put together, confident even. And he looked good in that sweater, really good.

After reading his words, about love and friendship and releasing the brakes, she felt sick inside, as if on the edge of a stomach bug. She went to the bathroom and doused her face in cold water. Because this wasn't supposed to be happening. Because Thatcher was not Kieran, and Kieran was the plan.

THATCHER

With the picture posted, Thatcher went to bed. But just as he was about to fall asleep, his door flew open.

A messy-haired Scout walked in. "What's the matter?" he asked as she made a sleepy beeline to his office chair.

She didn't answer.

"Are you scared?" he asked. She nodded yes.

"Want me to check your closet?" he said, used to her nightmare-induced treks to his room.

She shook her head no.

Thatcher had no choice. He got up, pulled the comforter off his bed, and placed it on the floor. "Here. You can sleep next to my bed."

He held it open as Scout slid in. "You don't need to be scared of anything," he said.

"I'm not scared of *anything*," she said. "I'm scared of everything."

Me too, Thatcher thought as he turned off the lights and crawled back into bed.

KAEYA

It was almost eleven, and she'd been on the phone with Kieran for nearly fifteen minutes...with her TS in check. Amazing!

"And then the studio security people just let us go," she finished.

"You know, you're a criminal, Kaeya. I shouldn't be talking to you." He laughed, and his voice was strong, and she drank it in like medicine.

"Thatcher's the guy in the meme, right?" he asked. He didn't call him the *Marry Me Martha Guy.* She appreciated that.

"Yeah, why?" she asked as she turned over and faced the ceiling.

"Just wondering," he said. She figured there was more to it than that, but she let it drop. The conversation had been perfect so far, and she wanted to get off the phone before her TS did something stupid.

"Hey, school tomorrow," she said with a yawn. "We should be getting to bed."

"Yeah, about that," he said. "I was wondering if you, um, wanted to grab a coffee before school? I need to make amends for my mocha latte mistake."

Morning was good. She had more control in the morning. "Sure. What time?" she answered.

"Meet me in the school parking lot at fifteen till, and we can walk over to LuLu's."

"We're walking?" she said.

"Yes, walking, so get a good night's rest. Big day tomorrow."

He wished her good night, and Kaeya told him sweet dreams. And when she hung up, an incredible epiphany rained down on the room. Tomorrow was the day.

She fell back onto her bed and hugged a pillow. She'd resisted her Thatcher impulses, and Kieran asked her out. Definitely a sign that she was doing the right thing.

So why wasn't she dancing around the room like a maniac?

Of course she was excited...but there was something else, a vague sense of melancholy, like she had just said good-bye to someone at the airport.

16

MONDAY

THATCHER

Scout grabbed the violets from the dashboard. The bouquet was simple and small and held together with a red rubber band.

"What are these for?" she said as she lifted them to her nose.

Thatcher looked over at her. "I'm asking a girl to the dance."

Scout bounced up and down in her seat. "Who?" she squealed.

"A friend from school. Kaeya," he confided.

"How are you gonna to ask her?"

"I'm just gonna wait for her before school, give her the violets, and ask her."

Scout tossed the violets back on the dash. "How about you give her a crown to wear?" she said. "And then you can take her to the dance in a horse and carriage, a silver one with sparkly lights."

"And where am I supposed to get a horse and carriage?"

"From a fairy godmother, silly," joked Scout. There was a huge grin on her face, one that Thatcher hadn't seen for a while.

He pulled up to the kindergarten gate, early. "Yeah, but she'll have to say yes first," he explained.

"You're nice, Thatcher," Scout said. "Of course she'll say yes."

Thatcher waved as Scout hopped out of the car and skipped happily onto the playground. She needed a happy ending. He hoped he could give her one.

KAEYA

"Yeah. I remember gummy bear vitamins!" said Kaeya as she warmed her hands on her cup of hot chocolate. "I used to eat those things like candy, until my mom started hiding the bottle."

"But didn't those bottles have those child safety caps on them?" asked Kieran as he ducked under a low-hanging branch.

"Curse the child safety caps!" she bellowed.

"I know, right?" He laughed. She loved the way he laughed, in short giggles like a little boy.

The morning had been awesome. The walk to LuLu's from the school parking lot. The random conversation. The way he'd offered her his Manchester City jacket when she said she was freezing. The way her TS had behaved. Yeah, Kieran was the one, definitely.

The only thing stressing her out now was that he hadn't asked her yet, and they were almost back at school.

"I can't believe Mrs. Candele assigned homework on Lanterns weekend," she complained as they headed back to school. Lanterns, the word of the day. She'd brought it up on purpose.

"I can believe it," said Kieran. "I have a soccer tournament in San Diego, for my club team."

Kaeya's shoulders dropped. Had she heard him wrong? "So wait. You're...going to be in San Diego this weekend?" she stuttered, trying hard to mask her disappointment.

He stared at the sidewalk and kicked a rock. "Yeah, State Cup. I couldn't get out of it," he said. He looked disappointed.

They walked silently for a while, their footsteps the only soundtrack.

"So how's the hot chocolate?" asked Kieran as they neared the school entrance.

"Good," she said with a hollow smile. But she was lying. It was the worst cup of hot chocolate she'd ever had. Because there would be no Lanterns...and she wondered if there ever would be.

THATCHER

A girl in a blue ASB shirt pulled a paper lantern from a huge box. "It's better to paint the base before you put the light bulb in," she explained as she handed it over.

Thatcher nodded as he placed it in his backpack. He'd figure out how to put the thing together later, after he asked Kaeya.

The Lanterns ticket line had taken longer than expected, and he was starting to panic. He needed to get to the front steps before she arrived, which, if Thatcher's calculations were correct, would be in about five minutes.

He clutched the violets and paced quickly toward the front of the school. The point of no return was upon him. In a matter of seconds, he'd know if Kaeya was more than a friend.

The front steps were crowded, so crowded that Thatcher couldn't reach the stairs. The entrance was usually packed in the morning, but this was beyond normal.

He slipped through several clumps of people in an attempt to reach the parking lot, and that was when he saw it, four tuxedo-wearing members of the glee club belting out a song in Italian. Students were cheering and holding up their phones to take videos. It was another Lanterns proposal. It had to be.

Thatcher moved over but still couldn't see. The crowd was going crazy now. She must have said yes. Standing on his tiptoes, he saw the couple hug, their heads obscured by the huge bouquet of roses the girl was holding. And it wasn't until the roses dropped and the guy let go that he understood...that the girl was Kaeya, and that he was too late.

Thatcher's eyes burned as he stepped back into a group of girls. "Hey!" scowled one of them as he brushed past.

But he couldn't hear her, couldn't hear anything. Because there were no more violets, no more Lanterns, no more Kaeya, only emptiness as he ran toward the parking lot.

Had this been yesterday's *worst day* competition, he would have won. Easily.

KAEYA

Saying he had a soccer tournament was brilliant, and Kaeya couldn't help but appreciate Kieran's lie. "You're so mean!" she scolded as she gave him another hug.

"Hey, I'm just getting even for your caramel latte fake-anger thing." He laughed as he shoved his hands in the pockets of his jeans.

"So we're even then," she conceded with a smile. They were going to be late, but she wasn't in a hurry to leave.

"I was thinking," began Kieran. "They're having this Lanterns Night on Thursday, at Paint Me Happy, so people can paint the base of their lanterns. It's like a fundraiser or something. Wanna go?"

Paint Me Happy. The pottery place. Kaeya had been there when she was little. "Of course," she said as she looked at her bouquet for the fiftieth time. Of course, the roses were a little over the top. But no one had ever given her flowers, and it was taking all of her strength not to cry.

Kieran jogged up the steps, two at a time. "It's a date then," he called. "But I'm warning you. I'm a soccer player, not an artist," he said.

The tardy bell rang, but Kaeya couldn't move. Her plan had worked, actually worked! She'd been asked to Lanterns, by Kieran. *Mrs. D, I so deserve an A*, she thought as she watched him disappear.

Smelling the roses a final time, she skipped steps to the top...where she found them, a tiny bouquet of violets wrapped in a red rubber band. They were trampled and broken, and she felt sorry for them, because she really liked violets...even better than roses.

THATCHER

Mrs. D looked up when Thatcher walked in. She looked puzzled, probably because he was over an hour late. "Is everything okay?" she asked as he shuffled past her desk.

"Yeah," he said. A lie. Nothing was okay, not a thing. He would have told Mrs. D the truth. In fact, he was feeling so miserable at the moment that he would have given her a play-by-play description. But Kaeya was there, sitting in her usual spot on the sofa. She smiled when he walked in.

Thatcher forced a happy greeting and hid behind a book, hoping beyond hope that she wouldn't talk to him. Even though he'd spent the last hour in his car trying to get a grip on his emotions, they were still wild animals.

"Tolstoy still?" she said after an intensely awkward minute. Thatcher wasn't sure. He looked at the top of the page. *Anna Karenina*. She was right.

"Yeah, it's kind of long," he said in the most *I'm not upset at all about you and Kieran going to Lanterns* kind of voice he could muster. It wasn't very convincing. He could tell by the way she was looking at him, like he was a lost puppy. He turned back to Tolstoy, but it didn't help. He could feel her trying to read him, as if he were the novel.

"Um, I saw you and Kieran this morning," he said. "Congratulations...on Lanterns."

She bit her bottom lip and sighed. "Do you really mean that?"

Thatcher squirmed in his seat. He tried to change the subject. "So where's Sam?"

Kaeya wasn't buying it. "I'm sorry," she said.

"S-sorry? For what?" he asked. But he knew the answer. She'd figured out the obvious, that he liked her, really liked her, more than just a friend.

"I've been thinking about the way we..." Shen stopped. She looked up as if the words were posted on the rafters, then shook her head as if they weren't.

She flipped the notebook on her lap closed and dropped it into her book bag. "I guess what I'm trying to say is, thanks...*HA HA*...for being so...*HA*...cool to me," she stammered as she got up to leave.

"Sure," he whispered as she walked past.

He wanted to call her back, to kiss her gently, to hold her close until every muscle calmed. But she wasn't his to hold. She was the book he'd never finish...and it was time to turn the page.

KAEYA

Kaeya fell onto her bed and screamed into a pillow. He'd looked so defeated, as if joy was no longer a word in the dictionary. And it was all her fault.

By hugging him, and taking him shopping, and holding his hand, she'd led him on. And now he was broken, all because her stupid emotional GPS got messed up.

She threw the pillow against the wall and tried to grab hold of herself. "You're going to Lanterns, girl," she said. "You worked too hard for this."

The words were comforting, at least a little. Cutting Thatcher loose was the right decision, for his sake and for hers. Her plan was working. She needed to stick to the plan.

Getting back on course would be easy. In a few days, Thatcher's suspension would be over. Until then, she'd avoid the Gallery. He'd forget her. She'd forget him. The end.

Kaeya stared up at the ceiling and noticed. The star stickers that glowed so bright at night seemed pale and powerless in the afternoon sun.

THATCHER

He'd spent the night numbing himself with game show reruns. And it was working. He hadn't cried. Not yet. And he wasn't going to. Every time a tear would show its ugly face, he'd bat it back with a vengeance. There would be no more teary-eyed *Marry Me Marthas* staring back at him from the mirror. Never again.

While a middle-aged insurance agent answered rapid-fire questions about Broadway musicals, his mother came in.

She held up a paper lantern. It was flat and still in the package. "I found this in the trash," she explained. "Do you want to talk about it?"

Tears. Again. He fought to hold them back. But then his mother sat next to him, muted the TV, and gave him a hug.

And he sobbed like he'd never sobbed before. And in between gasps for air, he told her. About how mad he was at Dad for ditching them, about how she'd checked out emotionally, leaving Thatcher and Scout to fend for themselves, and about *Marry Me Martha*.

And after his mother apologized profusely for being oblivious, he told her about Lanterns and Kaeya...and how he thought he loved her. And for the first time in months, Mom stepped out from behind her own pain and listened.

"You know what they say," she said when he was finished. "'Tis better to have loved and lost than never to have loved at all."

Thatcher wiped his nose with the sleeve of his shirt. "Do you really believe that?" he asked.

His mother paused. "No, not at all!" she said with a giggle. Her smile was infectious, and it reminded Thatcher of how much he'd been missing it.

"So how about we watch a depressing movie, cry our eyes out, and gorge ourselves on chocolate chip ice cream." She reached over and turned on the lights. "Then we'll sleep it off, wake up like the world is new, and get on with our lives."

Thatcher nodded in agreement. Ice cream sounded good.

KAEYA

The tics were horrible, the worst she'd seen all year. And she was confused, totally confused. She needed to talk to someone, to clear her head. She needed to talk to Thatcher.

But how selfish would that be? Calling someone who was crushing on you to meet some emotional need when you didn't intend to crush back. No, she wasn't going to be that person. Choosing Kieran meant a full Thatcher detachment, for his sake...and for hers.

THATCHER

Something was happening. Something insane. There were comments on his page, at least fifty.

Saw your quote about friendship last night and finally asked her to marry me. Thanx for the inspiration! (Toledo, Ohio)

Faith, hope, and love to the Marry Me Martha *guy, my online muse (Basel, Switzerland)*

Like the new look. You're adorable!!!!!! (Phoenix, Arizona)

After replying to as many comments as he could, he got an idea.

KAEYA

Thatcher looked different, his eyes confident, his stare strong. This time the quote was broken up and set in ten frames that hung in odd angles along a huge white wall. Thatcher looked sweet as he held the frame in the middle, the one that said *LOST* in huge letters.

Tennyson says it's better to have loved and lost than never to have loved at all. True or false?

Kaeya loved the idea of a question. And other people must have loved it too, because there were over a hundred thousand views and hundreds of comments.

My grandfather was married to my grandmother for sixty years, and when she passed away he said she was worth every tear, read one.

I caught my boyfriend making out with my best friend...and I despise the day I met him, said another.

The list went on and on, with people from all over the world weighing in. Thatcher was getting his fifteen minutes, and she was proud of him.

She wanted to call and congratulate him, but she fought the urge. Their friendship had wandered precariously close to the edge of love, and she needed to avoid the cliff.

17

TUESDAY

THATCHER

Mr. Blakely leaned forward on his desk and exhaled. Thatcher had just showed the principal the original *Marry Me Martha* meme, the one they used at the pep rally. The guy wasn't taking it very well.

"Had you told us immediately after the assembly, this entire mess could have been avoided," he moaned

"I know, but I'm telling you now," Thatcher answered. He was confident, far different than the weak-kneed student who'd sat quietly in this same office a few days earlier.

The principal nervously shuffled papers while Thatcher watched. "I assure you, the front office had no idea that your image was going to be used at the school-spirit assembly." He was apologizing without apologizing, just like a politician.

"So I'd like you to reconsider my suspension," requested Thatcher. The words were his mom's. She'd helped him map the whole conversation out after the movie.

More paper shuffling. A nervous sip of coffee. "Well, that's easier said than done," the principal muttered. "Quentin's parents were more than upset about the incident."

"And *my* mom's pretty upset too," Thatcher answered as he stood to leave. He reached across the desk and shook Mr. Blakely's hand. He had no idea what would happen next, but it didn't matter. He'd told his side of the story, and that felt awesome.

As he made his way out, the front office was a zoo, with stressed-out students, teachers, and parents jamming narrow halls. He pushed his way through the crowd until he reached the lobby. And that was where he saw him, a student sitting with his dad in the waiting room. It was Quentin.

Talk about timing, thought Thatcher as he watched Quentin fiddling with his phone. There were crutches leaning on the chair beside him. Was it difficult for him to walk?

Whether it was all those quotes he'd been reading about love or his talk with Mom, Thatcher wasn't sure, but a voice inside was telling him, *Time to move on.*

"Hey, Quentin," he called, his voice trembling.

Quentin looked up, a puzzled expression on his face. His father stood as if to protect him.

"I'm sorry...for hurting you," Thatcher started. "I totally lost it."

Quentin tilted his head, stared at Thatcher for a few seconds, then turned back to his phone. And at that moment, Thatcher felt a strange sensation. Strength. As if he'd won some invisible war.

KAEYA

She'd spent the majority of the day in the library, hiding out at a back table behind the reference section. Sure, it wasn't perfect, but she'd survived the day.

When three o'clock rolled around, she picked up her things and headed for the hall, the one Kieran usually took.

Her little detour paid off.

"Hey, friend," said Kieran as he tapped her on the shoulder.

She turned and acted surprised. "Well, hey back," she said as she gave him a hug. He always smelled so good, like aftershave. She drank it in.

"So what are you going to wear, you know, for color-coordination purposes?" he asked.

"Color-coordination purposes?" Kaeya laughed. "You sound like a fashion consultant or something."

Kieran didn't laugh back. "Seriously, what are you going to wear?" he asked again.

"In my daydreams, I'll be wearing a perfectly creative Youtopia dress. It's got vintage lace and looks amazing. But in reality...I have no idea."

"You should really get going on that," he said. He sounded like he was talking to a five-year-old. That bothered her.

They talked until the path parted ways.

"I'm late to practice," he said. "Talk to you later?"

"Of course," she said as she watched him leave.

Kaeya adjusted her book bag and headed to the parking lot. When she reached her car, she noticed something. Thatcher. He was standing next to a black Hyundai and talking to a girl, Fiona. Kaeya recognized her from language arts.

Thatcher seemed to be enjoying the talk, a lot. And why wouldn't he? She was perfectly beautiful and wore glasses that screamed CREATIVE! She probably even loved the same books as he did.

Kaeya should have been happy, like he always seemed when she talked about Kieran. But she definitely wasn't, and that bothered her. She hated jealousy, had no time for it.

Don't even go there, she told herself as slid into the car. Of course he'd be talking to other girls. He was a guy, a good-looking guy, a really gentle good-looking guy, more gentle than anyone she'd ever met.

She glanced in the rearview mirror. Still talking.

THATCHER

She'd come out of nowhere while he was on his way out. She'd been following his Instagram account, and she totally loved his memes.

Fiona. Why hadn't he noticed her before?

"I have to say. You're probably the *only* high schooler in the state of California that reads Amélie Sarchet." She smiled as she pushed her blond bangs away from her face.

"I haven't read a lot of her stuff. I just love that quote," he explained.

Fiona recited the lines from memory. "'There comes a time when the fear of being alone outweighs the fear of rejection.'"

An obscure French author, and Fiona knew who she was. Impressive.

"All of us in the Emily Dickinson club rave about your memes," she said. "It's like you're fighting back, with words."

Thatcher raised his eyebrows in disbelief. "Emily Dickinson club? Here on campus?"

"You're looking at the vice president," she said. "We meet on Fridays after school, mostly to share our own poetry. In fact, this weekend *we're having our first annual We're not going to Lanterns because we're too cool party at my house.*"

He liked the cadence of her voice. It was cute.

"In other words, we don't have dates, so we're going to wallow in our sorrows by acting deep and discussing depressing poetry," she continued. "Wanna come?"

"Wow, you make it sound so appealing," he joked. "What time?"

"Seven o'clock, or whenever," said Fiona. "Just show up if you want, or don't. No pressure."

Thatcher made sure to get her number. The party might be fun, definitely more fun than obsessing about Kaeya and Kieran dancing the night away.

He watched as Fiona drove off, then lifted his phone to make sure her number was still there. It was. And so was a text he'd missed. It was from Dad.

Wanna check out that new coffee place with me? Elevate? Tomorrow. Please!

Maybe it was the *Please* at the end, or maybe

Thatcher's attitude was changing, but Dad's tone seemed softer, humbler.

He stared down at the screen for a while. He was too tired to be angry.

Sure, he texted back.

KAEYA

Dad was fine, excited even, until the inevitable question.

"And he knows about your Tourette's?"

She shook her head in frustration. No, Kieran didn't know. Yes, she knew that a relationship should be built on honesty. No, she wasn't sure how she'd hide her TS during Lanterns.

The conversation grew heated, and angry words were exchanged. She spent the next hour in her room, listening to music, doing homework, feeling guilty about raising her voice.

Why didn't Dad get it? This mattered, more than anything. Even if her silver carriage turned back into a pumpkin and her dress turned to rags. It would all be worth it in the end. Right?

THATCHER

The Fiona thing was a distraction, like medicine to numb the pain. He tried to daydream about it, because he was hurting. But he was having a hard time because he kept thinking about Friday night, and Kaeya, and how much it would hurt to know she was with *him*.

"Just keep moving. One step at a time," he told himself as he looked through his journal of quotes for the topic of tonight's picture. The posts were easy at first, when he thought no one was watching. But now that his pictures had caught fire, he was becoming a perfectionist. Each one had to be deep, unique, artistic.

The pictures mattered now. What he had to say mattered. He mattered.

KAEYA

Too frustrated to concentrate, she put her calculus book down and searched for Thatcher's latest meme. His pictures had become a habit, one that she wasn't ready to give up.

Her heart slowed when she saw his dimly lit face. He was standing in the middle of the street, his hair blowing in the wind. His quote was written on a sheet this time, a sheet that flew out from his arms like a billowing parachute. The words and wrinkles, the way the street lamp illuminated the letters, it was beautiful, especially his calm eyes. She needed calm.

Love is a forever thing, read the caption. She'd never read Jenna Hardin, but she would now. Because her words felt true, and beautiful, and *so* like something that Thatcher would say.

She stared at his eyes, his sad, sweet eyes, and began to doubt herself, doubt everything. Sure, she liked

Kieran, a lot. But she wanted more than just a dance. She wanted a forever. But could Kieran give her that?

18

THATCHER

A misty rain swirled as Thatcher walked down the empty walkway. Mrs. D had let him leave early, to beat traffic, and he was more than happy to comply. He hated the Gallery. It reminded him too much of violets and the happy cadence of Kaeya's voice.

She hadn't showed for two days, and Thatcher knew why. He'd been ridiculously obvious about liking her, and Monday's conversation had been horrifically awkward. Who could blame her for wanting to avoid him?

He turned the corner and made his way past the field where the soccer team was finishing up laps. One of the players was sprawled out on the grass and pouring water on his head.

When Thatcher walked by, he looked up. "Hey," he called as he jogged up to the fence. "You're the meme guy, um, Thatcher. Right?" he said, still out of breath from his last-period workout.

Thatcher recognized him. It was Kieran. What did the guy want?

"Yeah, that's me," he said.

"I've been following your quotes. Kaeya told me about them. What do you got now, like four hundred thousand followers?" he asked.

"Something like that," Thatcher nodded.

The sound of thumping soccer balls and coaches' whistles punctuated the wet air as he waited for Kieran to say something. The guy was making him nervous.

"Look, I just wanted to say I'm sorry," Kieran finally blurted.

Thatcher bit his lower lip. Had Kaeya told him about his crush on her? Was this Kieran feeling sorry for him?

"Sorry?" said Thatcher.

"Yeah, for the whole *Marry Me Martha* thing."

More soccer kick thumps. A stereo blasting from the parking lot. Thatcher remained silent.

"I'm the one who fished your picture out of the trash, and I feel awful about it," he continued. "I was just joking around, you know, showing it to people and stuff. Then Quentin posted the meme, and everything went crazy."

Thatcher's muscles tensed. The anger was back, the same anger that put Quentin in the hospital...and he hated it. He closed his eyes and took a deep breath, then shrugged and stepped away.

"Apology accepted," he said. "Have fun at Lanterns."

KAEYA

She'd narrowed it down to two dresses: the white one she wore at Christmas and the one she'd bought on sale at Clarendon last summer. Kaeya had tried them on at least ten times each, but she still couldn't decide.

She dropped the dresses and sat down on the floor. The stress was getting to her. She'd been squealing and twitching all day. She'd even missed school because she could hardly walk without crashing into a wall. She needed to get a grip, or there'd be no Lanterns.

There was a knock on the door. She looked up. It was Dad.

"Can I come in?" he asked gently. She hadn't spoken to him since their argument. It was about time they did.

He came in and sat down on the floor with her.

"I'm sorry," he said with a shake of his head. "I worry too much."

With Dad, forgiveness was always easy. She reached over and gave him a hug.

"I wish you'd just trust me for once," she said.

"I do trust you," he answered. "But being a parent is like..." Her dad paused. He was tearing up.

"Is like what?" she said.

"It's like flying a kite. You build it, and you're proud of it, and you take it out and fly it every day. And you love that kite like you've never loved anything before. Then one day, the kite starts pulling away and pulling away, until you can barely hold on to it anymore.

"At first you think it's broken, that you've built it all wrong. And you get frustrated and hold on tighter. But then you realize, kites are meant to fly...and you let go."

Kaeya gave him another hug. "Dad, that's one of the most depressing metaphors I've ever heard," she said. "But I get it."

Dad laughed as he wiped a tear away. "So we having a garage sale?" he joked as he pointed to the pile of clothes on the floor.

"Just trying to pick out a dress," she answered.

"I see," he said as he picked one up. "You know, I may be able to help you with that."

Kaeya shook her head in mock exasperation as he walked out of the room. A fashion consultant he was definitely not.

A minute later he returned...with a bag behind his back. "I heard you needed this," he said as he handed it over.

She reached in and pulled out a dress, the Youtopia dress she'd been dreaming of. "Y-you've got to be kidding me!" she screamed as she practically tackled him at the door.

"B-but how?" she stammered as she held it up to her neck.

"A friend of yours stopped by when I was mowing the lawn. He gave me a picture of it, even gave me the store's address. Didn't know your size though. I checked the laundry to find that out."

"Who was it?" she asked, though she already knew.

"It was that boy, the one you filmed the movie with."

"Thatcher," she whispered.

"Yeah, that's him! He's a good guy," her dad said.

She looked down at the dress, its vintage sleeves soft in her hands.

"Yeah, he is," she said.

THATCHER

The scent of baked bread mixed with the smell of coffee. Elevate on Fifteenth Street had just opened, and it was Thatcher's first visit.

"They actually have tile that looks like wood now," Dad said. "It lasts a lot longer than conventional plank flooring."

Thatcher had been waiting for the right moment for nearly an hour now, but Dad wasn't leaving any space. His father's monologues about public transportation, traffic, and the various types of wood flooring were blocking the way, and it was time to push through.

"You haven't once asked how we're doing," Thatcher whispered when his father took a sip of water.

Mr. Kelly wiped his chin with a napkin. He looked flustered. "Okay?" he said, eyebrows raised. "So how are you all doing?"

"Oh, we've been doing *great*," Thatcher began, his voice trembling as he spoke. "For starters, Scout's been having nightmares. She pretty much comes into my room every night, sometimes shaking. Oh yeah, they took my school picture on the day you left. I looked like crap. And guess what? Now practically everyone in the free world has seen it."

Dad drummed his fingers on the table, like he always did when he was upset. Thatcher didn't care.

"And Mom's taken up a new hobby...crying," Thatcher added. "Kind of looks like she's been kicked in the stomach and can't catch her breath. I'm thinking it's probably because she *has* been kicked in the stomach. That's a simile, by the way, in case you didn't catch it."

More finger drumming. Faster this time. "Look, Thatcher, I'm hurting too, but this is our new reality as a family, and we're all going to have to learn to deal with it."

"You know, I used to think that Mom was weak, for caring too much, for always waiting by the phone for you to call, for crying. But now I'm starting to realize that she was the strong one. She made a choice to love you, to love this family, and she was willing to go down with the ship for it. Because that's what *real* love is, Dad...strong and unwavering and desperate."

"Lots of families survive divorces, Thatcher, and we will too," he explained. "Once I get a permanent place of my own, you and Scout can visit and..."

Thatcher stood, his hands trembling. "Dad, I love you, but what you're doing to us is selfish and totally messed up."

His dad yelled as Thatcher grabbed his sweatshirt and headed for the door. "You know I didn't drive all the way down here to be disrespected like this!"

And everyone in the coffee shop turned to look. Except Thatcher.

KAEYA

She stared at the dress hanging on her doorframe and smiled.

Thanks, Thatcher...for everything, she texted.

In a matter of seconds, he texted back.

No problem :)

She hung up and sighed.

THATCHER

He'd driven into LA for the picture, but the late-night trip was worth it.

He stared down at his phone and read the quote again.

There is no remedy for love but to love more. —
Henry David Thoreau

It was perfect.

KAEYA

She saw Thatcher's meme. He was sitting in cool looking coffee shop looking pensive, a thought bubble Photoshopped above his head.

There is no remedy for love but to love more. —
Henry David Thoreau

It was perfect.

19

THATCHER

Sam shook Thatcher's hand when he got up off the sofa, which was weird. "Hang in there Thatcher," he said as he let go. He nervous, hollow, like he was in pain, which was also weird.

"You too," he answered as Sam began to leave.

Mrs. D met Sam at the door. "God bless you, friend," she said as she gave him a hug. The scene was all so serious and somber, and Thatcher spent the rest of the day wondering what was up.

The gallery was no longer a refuge, it was like a party that had ended, an empty shell awash in memories and dirty paper plates. With Sam gone, he read, and napped, and read some more. Until the bell rang and it was time to go home. He *needed* to go home.

He decided to leave through the main part of campus this time, through the science building and out the front gate. That way was more crowded, but the Gallery had been dead quiet and needed some noise.

Halfway across the quad, he saw Fiona. "So have you decided whether or not to hang out in the land of the nerds on Friday?" she asked as she walked over to him.

Fiona was cute, in a different kind of way, but the thought of hanging out with a bunch of people he didn't know seemed awkward. "I'm not so good with strangers," he admitted.

"Well, I'm not a stranger." She smiled. "Besides, everyone knows you. You're like a meme rock star."

Her big, round eyes were pleading, and he definitely didn't want to be alone on Lanterns night. "Okay," he said.

Fiona looked openly ecstatic, and Thatcher couldn't help but smile.

KAEYA

Paint Me Happy was chaotic, with overly affectionate couples, groups of friends, and ASB members crowding around long tables and yelling to be heard over the music.

Kaeya and Kieran were lucky enough to have snagged a little kids' table in the corner, the only nongroup table in the place. The mini chairs were built for toddlers, which meant Kaeya's and Kieran's knees were practically touching their chins as they painted. But at least they were alone.

"Oops!" said Kaeya after smearing a blob of light-blue paint on the paper part of her lantern.

Kieran smiled. "I like it. Looks kind of Picasso-ish," he said as he worked on a white cloud.

Kaeya coughed as she tried to suppress another tic. "Yeah, but we're only supposed to paint the base," she said as she tried to wipe it off.

The night was off to a rough start, with two bathroom escapes and one trip to the car to "get something."

Suddenly, Kieran pointed his paint brush at her purse. "You're phone is ringing," he yelled over the crowd.

She wiped her hands on a paper towel and grabbed her purse off the floor. "It's probably my dad," she said.

The phone was there, somewhere, probably buried at the bottom. She started dumping items on the table until she finally found it.

"Yup, Dad," she said as she looked at the screen. "But he can wait."

She turned back to the table, where the contents of her purse had formed a small mountain.

"Haldol?" asked Kieran as he picked up a plastic bottle.

Her TS meds! She'd taken them out for the world to see.

"Are you sick or something?" he asked.

Her first instinct was to make up a story about an easier ailment, a cold, back pain, maybe pneumonia, but her Tourette's wouldn't let her.

"Arrr! Arr!" she cried, trying desperately to force the sound into a cough. But it was hopeless. Kieran was staring, like he'd seen a ghost.

And that was the moment she knew. If Kieran was the *one,* he'd have to love all of her, not just the parts she wanted him to see. It was time...time to let him know.

Kaeya's heart pounded as she fumbled for the words. "Kieran," she said, "there's something I need to tell you."

THATCHER

"Shhh," Thatcher told Scout. "Mom's gonna hear us and make you go to bed."

"But you're not following the rules," she whisper-yelled. "You can't pick up the phone until you've guessed who your crush is."

"Okay, but there's no way you're beating me to the Princess Prom," he said as he rolled the pink dice.

Playing Dream Crush with Scout on the eve of Lanterns was not Thatcher's idea of a good time. But his sister wasn't scared when she shuffled into his room tonight—she was teary eyed and sad, and Thatcher would have done almost anything to cheer her up.

"Oh yeah. I'm gonna win," he yelled as he landed on the heart with a question mark on it. "I predict that *Genevieve* is my dream crush."

"Pick up the phone and press seven!" squealed Scout. Hearing the messages at the end of the game was her favorite part.

"I'm coming, Genevieve!" he joked as he pressed the button and waited for his dream crush to answer.

Hi, this is Ashley. I thought you'd never call, answered an overly dramatic female. *I've been crushing on you forever. Hey, I was wondering, do you want to take me to the Princess Prom?*

"Never!" shouted Thatcher into the plastic receiver. "Genevieve is my true love! I love her more than puppies, and Hello Kitty, and even more than...Cheerios!"

The joke was stupid, but Scout laughed hysterically, which gave him an idea. He got up and rummaged through his desk for a marker. A line had popped into his head, and he needed to write it down before he forgot. When he finally found a marker, he scribbled the line in large letters.

Love is playing silly games because it makes her laugh.

With Dream Crush in view, he pulled Scout close and snapped a picture.

KAEYA

The dress fit like it was meant to be, like Lanterns was meant to be. She smiled as she looked in the mirror and allowed herself to be happy.

THATCHER

The *playing silly games* quote got a lot of comments, especially on Instagram. The third one down caught his attention.

Check this out, it said, along with the hashtag *#thethatcherresistance*. Underneath was a link to an Imogene Spyres vlog. Being that Imogene was a decently famous British YouTuber, he was shocked by what he saw.

The vlog chronicled Imogene's trip to a concert in New York, a Martha Baines concert. The video, which lasted about five minutes, ended with Cassandra and a group of five or six friends pressed against the stage and holding up signs. *Time to apologize Martha*, said one. *Memes are people too* and *Marry Me Thatcher*, said the others.

As Martha Baines took the stage, Imogene smiled into the camera. "I'm suffering through this for you, Thatcher," she screamed over the music. "I hate country music."

Another girl interrupted from behind. "Hold the sign higher!" she called. "She's looking at us!" And the video ended.

Thatcher shook his head, then watched it again.

KAEYA

The text came at eleven. Nine words.

> *Can't make it to Lanterns tomorrow. Soccer*
> *...so sorry.*

She'd known it would come. Because of Kieran's disturbed look when he heard the word Tourette's. Because of the fake smiles and awkward small talk that followed. Because Kieran left early with his eyes to the ground.

She read the message a second time and a third, hoping the words had somehow morphed into something less cruel. But the underlying message was always the same. *You're flawed, and I'm too embarrassed to be seen with you.*

That feeling of hope she'd had since transferring—that life could be normal, that love was a tangible possibility, that happy endings existed beyond the pages of fairy tales—had vanished in a feeble puff of smoke. And now there was nothing left to do, nothing left to say...nothing.

So she crumpled onto the floor like old laundry, and wept, and slept, and wept some more, until a sliver of gray poked an ugly finger through the blinds, reminding her...

It was the morning of Lanterns, and she was all alone.

20

THATCHER

Kaeya never showed, neither did Sam, making the Gallery quiet, too quiet. Thatcher had way too much time to think.

Would Kieran pick Kaeya up in a limo? Would they kiss? Thatcher was obsessing so much he hadn't noticed Mrs. D.

"Congratulations," she said as she sat across from him.

He looked up, eyebrows raised. "Congratulations? For what?" he asked.

"For being a free man," she answered. "I just talked to Mr. Blakely. Your suspension's been suspended."

His suspension was over? Thatcher didn't understand. "But I've only served eleven days," he said. "And what about the project?"

"You're off the hook, Thatcher," she said. "And as for the project, you're done. What is it now, five hundred thousand likes? Crazy impressive, my friend. And I've seen all the comments. You've used your fifteen minutes quite nicely."

Thatcher fell back on the sofa. "Oh my gosh. This is like—

"Sick? Awesome? Rad?" she interrupted.

"Yeah, something like that." He laughed. "And thanks for believing me on day one."

"You're very welcome," she said. "It's going to be lonely around here without you guys."

"At least you still have Kaeya and Sam."

Mrs. D stood and straightened her skirt. "Well, Kaeya seems to be avoiding us lately. And Sam's health is going to keep him out of school for a while."

"Why? Is he stressing out again?"

"Stressing out?" she said.

"Yeah, having panic attacks. You know, about his schoolwork and stuff."

"Is that what he told you guys? That he was here because of panic attacks?"

Mrs. D leaned forward with an intense stare, her hands on her knees. "Thatcher, I'm not sure if I'm supposed to be telling you this, but Sam has a congenital heart defect. He's having triple bypass surgery this weekend."

Triple bypass surgery? The words sounded a lot like *car accident* or *brain tumor*.

"The plan was to let Sam come to the Gallery when he needed to reduce his stress levels, and wait until summer for surgery. But now his doctors are saying that he can't wait that long."

His mind was spinning, like he'd spent too long on a math problem. He buried his head in his hands.

"It's his fifth surgery, Thatcher," she consoled. "He'll be okay."

The words seemed hollow, and Thatcher could tell she didn't believe them. And for some reason, he didn't believe them either.

KAEYA

She'd been there since lunch. Her head resting on the kitchen table. A cold bowl of soup keeping it company.

Her dad, who'd stayed home to be with her, rubbed the back of her neck. "You'll feel better by Monday," he said.

"No, I won't," she sobbed. "I'm not going back."

"Sweetheart, you're just upset. Wait a few weeks before deciding anything."

It was strange, her father telling her to stay at Glen Canyon, while she wanted out. She sat up and blew her nose. "I'm going back to Centennial."

"Preciosa, there'll be other boys and other dances."

"Dad, you don't understand. This wasn't about a boy or a dance. It was about a million other things, like not being known as the weird girl, and being normal, and making friends. And I totally failed, at all of that."

When she was finished, she broke into another chorus of sobs.

Her father placed his hand on hers. "But you did make a friend," he said softly.

The room grew silent as Kaeya let the words sink in. He was right. She'd made a friend, a good one. But she hadn't been a very good friend back.

THATCHER

Thatcher hated everything about hospitals. The smell of urine. The sound of beeping machines. They reminded him of the fragility of life, a depressing concept he'd picked up from reading too many Victor Hugo novels.

Mrs. D had told him which hospital. She'd even let him leave early. "Your teachers won't be expecting you back in class until Monday," she'd said with a sly smile.

After a couple of wrong turns, he finally found Sam's room. He took a deep breath and stepped in.

With the heart monitor beeping and an IV attached to his arm, Sam looked frail, as if he'd morphed into a skeleton overnight.

"Hey, dude!" Thatcher called as he approached the bed.

Sam jumped, startled by the surprise, and Thatcher worried that the shock would mess him up even more.

"Panic attacks, my foot," he said. "Why didn't you say anything?"

Sam shrugged. "I don't know," he mumbled.

"Don't like drama, I guess."

Thatcher took a seat on the chair next to the head, and Sam pressed a button to tilt it up.

"So when's the surgery?" he asked.

"Early tomorrow morning."

"You scared?"

"A little. Waiting's always the worst part." Sam's breathing was heavy, like he'd just run the mile.

"I can hang with you tonight, if you want."

"Thanks, but I'll be all right," Sam said. "My mom and sister are here. They just went across the street to grab something to eat."

Thatcher nodded.

"So, you going to Lanterns?" Sam asked.

"Nah," Thatcher mumbled, embarrassed by the question. "But I did get asked to an official *anti*-Lanterns party, by this girl named Fiona."

"Fiona! I know her. She's awesome!" Sam beamed. "You're going, right?"

"I was, but every time I think about Fiona, my brain keeps defaulting back to—"

"Kaeya," Sam interrupted.

"Well, yeah," Thatcher answered. "I'm still not over her, I guess."

Sam propped himself up some more and moved the tubes of his IV to out of the way. "I texted her this morning," he said.

"You did?"

"Yeah, I asked if she was excited about tonight, and she texted back, *Not going.*

Not going to Lanterns? Thatcher almost fell out of his chair. "Really?" he said. "I wonder what happened."

"Don't know. I asked, but she never texted back."

A nurse came in to grab something, and Thatcher stepped out of the way.

"Probably Kieran's fault," Sam continued when she was gone. "I have no idea what she saw in him." Sam closed his eyes, and Thatcher wondered if he should leave. "I'm surprised you hung on to her for as long as you did," Sam said. "You must have a high tolerance for pain."

"Either that or I'm stupid."

Sam laughed. "Not stupid. In love."

"I couldn't help it. Her smile was like this tractor beam sucking me into the vortex. And her smile and her stupid sense of humor were...Okay, now I'm really sounding like Sam Baldwin."

"*Sleepless in Seattle*! You watched it." Sam grinned and grimaced at the same time .

"Yup. With my mom the other night. Awesome movie."

"What did I tell you!" said Sam as he eased back on his pillow and grimaced. He was hurting.

"Get better soon so we can finish your movie trailer," said Thatcher as he turned to leave.

Sam coughed. "Already done."

"What do mean? We didn't even finish the last scene."

"Didn't need it. I'll send you a copy."

Another nurse walked in, making the tiny room even more tiny. Thatcher stepped aside as she brushed past. "So, um, good luck tomorrow," he said.

Sam closed his eyes. "You should talk to her," he said with a feeble wave.

Thatcher paused. "Maybe...someday," he answered.

"Well, take your time, but hurry up," teased Sam. Another movie line.

The nurse was talking as he left, talking to Sam like he was a lost little kid. And as Thatcher walked toward the elevator, he couldn't help but think that he was...that they all were.

KAEYA

There had always been magic. Dreams that somehow always came true. Still, small voices whispering in her ear to go this way or that way, as if there was a purpose, a reason for everything that happened on earth.

But tonight she wasn't sure.

She glanced at the clock. The couples would be arriving now, checking in their coats, moving onto the dance floor, pointing up at the starry night.

The TV was on downstairs. She could hear it through the bedroom door. Her father had begged her to watch a movie with him, but she'd refused. She wanted to ache alone.

She lay in the dark until a car pulled onto her street, its headlights bathing the room in white. It pulled up to the curb.

She sat up as the car's door slammed shut. *One of the neighbor's friends*, she thought at first. But then there was another sound, a voice. Was someone calling her name?

She got up and moved toward the window. Someone was on her lawn, kneeling down next to a lantern, a paper lantern that was actually starting to float upward...until it burst into a ball of flames.

THATCHER

"No, no, no!" Thatcher screamed as the flaming lantern began to list. Dumping his dad's torch on the sidewalk, he scrambled after the lantern as it crashed down on a clump of hydrangeas. He grabbed an edge in an attempt to fling it onto the lawn. But now a bush was on fire.

He grabbed his head in horror and scanned the front yard in search of a hose, but couldn't find one. He took off his jacket in the hopes of smothering the flames, but before he could begin, a fire extinguisher–toting figure emerged. Mr. Garay.

Streams of white foam blasted the flames into a cloud of white smoke.

"I...I'm so sorry," squeaked Thatcher as he stared at the smoldering hydrangea.

Kaeya's father turned, and Thatcher waited for the lecture. But Mr. Garay didn't speak, because he was leaning over his knees and laughing in huge bellowing gasps. He was soon joined by his daughter, who was staring down at the scene from the porch.

"Y-you said you liked the flying lanterns, like the ones in China," Thatcher explained when the giggling died down.

"Yeah, but I'm not really into the exploding ones," she said as she joined him on the lawn.

She was smiling, but her eyes were puffy and red. She'd been crying.

"I'll totally pay for the bush, Mr. Garay," he said as he knelt down to pick up the ashes.

Mr. Garay put his arms on Thatcher's shoulders and gave him a shake. "No worries, my friend," he answered. "I was going to get rid of that bush anyway."

Thatcher was suddenly glad that it was Kaeya's dad, not his own, on the end of the fire extinguisher. "No, seriously, I'll plant a new one," he said.

"You can pay me back by taking my mopey daughter away for the evening." He laughed as he headed back to the house. "Be back by eleven thirty."

Before Thatcher could apologize again, he was gone. Kaeya and Thatcher were alone.

They stood in the cold for a while and took turns kicking lines in the white foam. Dressed in pj bottoms and a tank top, Kaeya was shivering. So he put his jacket over her shoulders. She pulled the jacket close and smiled again, a good sign.

"So besides an overwhelming urge to destroy your shrubbery"—he smiled—"there was another reason I drove over here."

Kaeya crossed her arms and tilted her head to one side. Adorable.

"I know it's kind of late," he said, "but do you, um, want to go to Lanterns...with me?"

KAEYA

The answer was easy. "No way," she said as she toed the charred lantern remains on the lawn.

Thatcher looked heartbroken, his bow tie crooked and his face mortified in the moon's dim glow.

"I'm so sorry. That didn't come out right!" she explained. "I would absolutely *love* to go anywhere with you tonight, anywhere that doesn't involve floating lanterns or crowds of any kind. I look like a mess."

"Okay, I'll rephrase the question then. Kaeya Garay, who does not look like a mess, would you like to go anywhere else but Lanterns with me tonight?"

"Yes," she answered softly as she hugged him, tightly.

"One condition though," he said when she let him go. "You have to wear your new dress. I spent way too many hours online trying to remember which one you showed me."

Kaeya smiled. "Sure," she said.

His eyes were warm and kind, which made her want to hug him again. But that could wait until later. She didn't want to keep a friend waiting.

THATCHER

He held the door open for her. "Hey, where's your car?" she asked as she slid in.

"I took my mom's," he said. "That way there's no risk of blowing up on the freeway."

She pulled on her seat belt and smiled. "That's probably a good idea, considering you nearly burned my house down with your flaming lantern of death."

He checked for traffic and pulled onto the road.

"Seriously though," he said, "my car's fourteen years old. Breaking down is not really what I had in mind for tonight."

"At least we'd have a great first-date story." She laughed.

First date. The words nearly gave him a heart attack. "So is this like officially our first date?" he asked.

She turned to face him. "Well, I guess...if you want it to be."

KAEYA

She stared out the window and wondered. Was he just feeling sorry for her?

"You know, you don't have to do this," she said.

"Do what?" he answered.

"This whole *taking me out because my heart's been broken* thing."

Thatcher braked to a stop in the middle of the street. "Kaeya, this isn't about me feeling sorry for you," he said. "This is about me being blown away because there's an amazingly beautiful girl sitting in the passenger seat of my car."

Kaeya blushed.

THATCHER

A row of yellow streetlights illuminated her face. Her perfectly painted lips, her pale skin—she was art, living art, and only inches away.

Don't touch, Thatcher thought to himself as he drove aimlessly through the night. *She needs a friend, not a boyfriend.*

He'd asked her about Kieran, and she was telling him. About her date. About how horrified he looked when she'd told him about her TS. About the text that tore her apart.

They stopped at a red light, and Kaeya turned toward the window to hide her tears. He reached over and awkwardly patted her shoulder, like she was a cat.

Don't even try to kiss her, he thought as he breathed in her perfume.

The light turned green, and Kaeya turned. "Let's talk about something else," she said softly. "So where are we going?"

The truth was, Thatcher had no idea where they were going. He'd been driving aimlessly for the last twenty minutes. "I don't actually know," he admitted as they turned onto a freeway.

"Take your time," she said as she looked into the rearview mirror and checked her makeup.

He wanted to tell her that she already looked beautiful, but he didn't. Too flirty.

Headlights lined the freeway like strings of pearls as Thatcher drove through the Canyon. He saw the sign for Skyline Drive, the exit before Wisteria Lake. And it came to him, like a happy bolt of lightning. Skyline Trail. The first lookout point. Why hadn't he thought of it earlier?

He swerved across three lanes of traffic and exited just in time.

Kaeya gave him a curious look.

"I have an idea," he said before she could ask. "I hope you don't mind walking a little."

KAEYA

The trail was dark, and she wanted more than anything to grab Thatcher's hand for protection. But she didn't want to look like a girl on the rebound desperate for anyone to latch on to, so she didn't.

The path was getting steep now. Luckily, she'd chosen to wear black combat boots with the dress she was wearing, perfect for hiking.

"Um, lonely dirt road? No one in sight? This is starting to feel a little too much like a horror movie," she complained as they reached another switchback. "You aren't planning on murdering me and cutting me up into little pieces, are you?"

Thatcher laughed. "Hey, you're the one who wanted to go somewhere where there were no people."

"When I said I wanted to be alone, I meant corner table at Starbucks alone, not climb into the hills like *Survivorman* alone."

She pushed past him, and Thatcher picked up his pace to keep up. "Trust me," he said. "You're gonna love this."

"Um, as I recall, last time I trusted you, we almost got arrested."

"Okay, *A*, that whole Paradigm Studios thing was Sam's idea, and *B*, this is a state park, so we're not trespassing."

The first ridge was in reach now, its straight edge illuminated by a huge silver moon. And she could hear it now. Music. Flowing upward from the valley below.

THATCHER

Her face went from curiosity to confusion to comprehension.

"We're near the lake, aren't we?" she said.

Thatcher quickened his pace. "You'll see," he teased. "We're almost at the lookout point."

The last yards of the trail bent upward at a ridiculous angle. Kaeya was slipping, so he offered his hand. Her palm was warm, even in the evening chill, and he held on a few seconds longer than necessary. She didn't pull away, even when they reached the top.

They were several hundred feet above Wisteria Lake, but they could see everything. The strings of light bulbs hanging crisscross over a dance floor. Couples the size of ants swaying to old-school music. Glowing lanterns, hundreds of them, bobbing like fireflies near the water's edge.

"Welcome to Lanterns," he said.

And Kaeya was crying when she hugged him, her tears falling on the back of his neck.

KAEYA

Louis Armstrong. "As Time Goes By." She recognized the song from an old movie.

"I had a dream about Lanterns," she said as sat crisscross on the ridge. "I was in my dress watching everyone dance. And everything was warm and beautiful and fairy-tale perfect." Thatcher leaned back on his elbows, his eyes to the sky and his feet dangling over the edge. He nodded to show he was listening, but didn't interrupt.

"And when I woke up, I felt like the dream was a sign. You know, like I was meant to go to Lanterns, like I was supposed to be with Kieran."

"You mean, like a prophecy?"

She shook her head. "I know, crazy. Right?"

Thatcher threw a piece of grass into the wind. "Not really. I mean, look. You *are* at Lanterns, in your dress, watching everyone dance."

There was something in his eyes as he spoke, something intensely adorable, something that made her want to beg for forgiveness for having let go of his hand in the theater parking lot. He was right, about the dream, about Lanterns, about everything. And as he said it, she began to feel something she hadn't felt in a long time. Peace. Hope. The sense of calm that comes when you start to believe in magic again.

She wanted more than anything to make up for lost time, to turn and kiss him like she should have back then. But that would seem too forward. So she didn't.

But Thatcher did.

Putting both arms around her, he pulled her close and kissed her, gently, as if her face was porcelain. Then suddenly, he pulled away. "I...I'm so sorry," he apologized. "It's too early, and I didn't..."

"Shh," she said, pressing a finger against his mouth. "I'm the one who's sorry, for taking so long." And she leaned into his lips once more.

And when she stopped, he kissed her again, twice more. And with each kiss she felt a peace, knowing that Thatcher was her closest friend, knowing that each kiss could be trusted.

With the moon's reflection smiling from the surface of the lake, she leaned into his shoulder, and he rested his cheek on the top of her head. And then they listened. Quietly.

The song was old. Probably Frank Sinatra again."Wanna dance?" she asked.

"I don't know how," he whispered.

"Thatcher! Who's gonna notice?" she answered as she grabbed his hands.

"You will." He blushed.

"Well, your secret's safe with me," she said as she pulled him close. And they swayed through that song, and the next, until they knew nothing but the lake, and the stars, and the moment...and the moment was theirs.

THATCHER

Clouds had moved over the moon, but he could still count the freckles on her nose. He kissed them, and she smiled. They'd been talking for nearly two hours, and now the dance was winding down. But he didn't want to move, didn't want to spoil what had become his best day, and minute, and second.

"So how did you discover this place?" she asked as she looked up from his shoulder."I used to come up here a lot with my dad, when I was little. And he'd always announce that we were going to hike to the top of the trail, which is like another couple of miles up. I'd get all excited and pack snacks and stuff. But by the time we reached the first lookout, he'd be too tired, and we'd always have to turn around."

Thatcher felt her fingers under his sleeve. "How sad," she said as she rubbed her thumb on the inside of his forearm.

"I got used to it."

"You shouldn't have to get used to that."

"It's not like he meant to let me down. He just never really got it. To him, love is this epic feeling, this firework that shoots up and disappears in a puff of smoke."

Kaeya reached for his hand, her fingers intertwined with his. "And what's love supposed to be?" she asked.

"Well, it's definitely a feeling," he began. "But it's more than that. I guess it's like a choice. You choose to love someone, whether the feelings are there or not...and then the feelings come back, stronger than ever."

A strand of hair blew into Kaeya's face. She pushed it away. "You bleed poetry," she said.

"I know. I'm a living Hallmark card."

She smiled as she let her forehead drop against his chest.

The last notes of the night were fading now as ant-sized couples began moving off the dance floor. Near the shore, someone was giving a speech, probably about cleaning up. Lanterns was over.

After brushing the dirt off the back of his jeans, he reached into his pocket. "Um, I almost forgot," he said as he pulled out a tiny bouquet of violets. "They were supposed to be part of the whole 3-D flying-lanterns experience."

Kaeya held them in her hands like a holy relic. "I'll climb to the top of the trail with you next time," she promised as she kissed him on the cheek.

And Thatcher believed her.

KAEYA

They pulled up to the curb with three minutes to spare. She leaned over and kissed him on the cheek.

"Good night. Now go." He laughed.

But she wasn't ready. Not yet. "Thatcher, about Kieran," she started.

"It's all right. I get it."

"No, you don't. Because I didn't. Not until this week."

He turned off the engine. "Okay," he said.

"Um, how can I say this? It was like...like Kieran was a side effect of my TS, like some weird tic that I had to let out before moving on."

Thatcher looked down at the steering wheel and smiled. "Understood," he said as he reached over Kaeya's lap and opened the door. "Now, go already. Your dad's gonna think I'm totally irresponsible."

"Because you *are* irresponsible. You practically burned down our house," she said, followed by a quick "I love you."

"We'll, you're cruel and merciless, and I love you back," he answered.

She reached into the car and gave his hand a quick squeeze before dashing up the stone walkway to her house. It was 11:38. She'd made it home in time...almost.

THATCHER

The picture showed Thatcher, staring up at the stars, his sleeping bag in the yard.

> *There's an unfortunate side effect of love, an infinite ache that keeps us up at night.*
> —*Georges Toquemelle*

There was more to Toquemelle's quote, a lot more, and Thatcher had wanted to write it all. But the frame was only so big and his heart too full. So he left it at one line. One line to express how he felt. Too much but not enough

KAEYA

Snapchat. Instagram. Twitter. Hundreds of thousands
would see the meme, but this one was for her. She ran her
finger across the words as if they were magic...because
they were.

THATCHER

It was technically tomorrow when the text arrived. Four
simple words that made his head spin.

I can't sleep either :)

21

SATURDAY

KAEYA

Sam Min-Jun Park died as the sun rose. It was during surgery, so he wasn't in any pain. At least that was what Mrs. D said when she called.

"I'm so sorry, sweetheart," she said. "I know you two were good friends."

The words *were* and *friends* made it seem like Sam no longer existed, which seemed wrong, because he'd texted her yesterday, and she'd talked to him a few days before that.

Mrs. D's voice seemed distant as she continued to talk.

There was an address. Would she like to send a card?

Sure.

There would be a memorial assembly at school on Tuesday. Would she like to speak? She had no idea.

The last thing Mrs. D said was sorry, as if Sam's death was her fault. Kaeya told her thank you. The call ended. And the world was different.

A cartoon whispered from a distant TV. A neighbor's lawnmower roared from next door. A motorcycle raced down the street. Saturday morning was happening as always, but Sam Min-Jun Park wasn't a part of it, would never *be* part of it again.

THATCHER

A VW Bug pulled up to the curb. Kaeya. Rushing to the driver's side, he opened her door.

Her face was pale, her eyes lost. "I needed a hug," she said as she fell into his arms.

So he held her, long and hard, so hard that Thatcher could feel her tears soaking through his T-shirt. And with every gut-wrenching sob, he kissed the top of her head and wiped her tears with his thumbs.

KAEYA

Thatcher rubbed her arms. They'd been outside for almost an hour, and she welcomed the warmth.

"They're having a memorial assembly at school," she said.

"When?" he asked.

"Tuesday. Mrs. D asked me to speak."

"Are you gonna do it?"

Kaeya looked away to stifle a tic. "I'm not sure."

"Worried about your Tourette's?"

She nodded. The whole school would notice.

"But I probably should," she said.

"You can say no. Sam would understand." He used the present tense. She liked that.

"I know he would, but I don't want to be selfish. He was my first friend at Glen."

The sun ducked behind a cloud, making the temperature drop even more.

"Wanna come in?" Thatcher asked.

She hesitated. His mom would be on the other side of that door, and Kaeya had rushed over without thinking. Her hair was a mess. She was still wearing her PJ bottoms. Hardly the first impression she wanted to make.

But it was too late now. He was already leading her up the walkway, opening the dark-blue door, walking in.

Ready or not, here I come.

THATCHER

Thatcher's mother was standing in the kitchen. Besides the girls who'd come over to work on group projects, this was the first time he'd brought a *girl* home, a monumental event in the Kelly home.

"Mom, this is my friend Kaeya," he said.

Kaeya's eyes were still red from crying, but she managed a beautiful smile. "Hi," she said with a shy wave. "Sorry. I'm a bit of a mess."

"No apologies necessary," Mom said as she pulled Kaeya into a hug. "I'm so sorry about your friend."

More tears from Kaeya, then from Mom, who was of the belief that crying was contagious. Thatcher dashed upstairs for a box of Kleenex.

When he returned, the conversation had moved to

the kitchen table. Scout was there, hiding behind Mom's back.

"You know what always makes me feel better?" Mom said. "Cookies."

"Yay! Chocolate chip!" screamed Scout as Mom headed to the pantry and pulled out a bag of flour.

Kaeya and Thatcher watched *Full House* reruns in the living room while Scout and Mom baked. Mostly though, they talked, about Sam, about Lanterns, about how Tolstoy was less complicated than he'd thought.

And when the cookies were done, they moved back into the kitchen, where Scout talked everyone's ear off, and Mom asked Kaeya to stay for pizza.

Thatcher had expected Mom to like her, but not this quickly. He smiled as he watched them chat, like family.

"We need milk," Mom announced as she placed a second plate of cookies on the table.

When Thatcher walked over to the refrigerator to grab some, he noticed the picture of Dad on the door. He was smiling as he held up a fishing rod. And Thatcher couldn't help but feel sorry for him.

Because Dad was missing this...missing the future.

KAEYA

It was late. She hoped he was still awake. *Thanks for being patient while I figured things out*, she texted.

THATCHER

He ditched the T-shirt for a button-up. Martha Baines didn't need any more publicity. He checked the picture again, the one they'd taken together while up at Skyline.

Love is always worth the wait. Always —Me

22

SUNDAY

KAEYA

She'd gotten to church early so she could sit in the main auditorium and pray for Sam, for the memorial assembly, and for his family, who'd need lots of hugs in the months ahead.

And if you could give me a hug yourself, she whispered. *I could really use one.*

The choir was taking the stage now. She looked at her watch. Ten. Time to retreat to the baby room. She picked up her purse and stood as the music began to play. And that was when she felt it, a still, small voice in her heart.

Stay.

She stared out at the vast crowd. She'd been vocalizing all morning. She'd annoy them.

Stay.

But the music would eventually die down, and the auditorium would grow quiet. She'd interrupt the opening prayer.

Stay.

Kaeya looked over at the exit. She was tired of the crying babies' room, tired of the Gallery, tired of hiding. If she couldn't be herself here, then she couldn't be herself anywhere.

She sat down again, bowing her head as a new wave of vocalizations began. "*HA, HA, HA!*"

A little kid pointed. A trio of junior high boys giggled. An elderly woman across the aisle looked angry. But she stayed. Until the music was over and the room grew quiet. Until the pastor began to pray. Until she felt an arm wrap gently around her shoulders.

Shocked at this unwelcome invasion of privacy, she pulled away. But then she saw his eyes, kind and caring and embarrassed all at once. Thatcher's.

"I-I'm so sorry. I didn't mean to freak you out," he whispered as he gave her a quick kiss. "Your dad told me I'd find you here."

She didn't say anything, just placed her hand in his and leaned on his shoulder. And for the millionth time that weekend, the tears began to fall.

THATCHER

Poki Kat was packed, as the sushi place always was at lunchtime. But they didn't mind the fifty-minute wait. Not at all.

They found a bench by the fountain outside. Perfect.

"To speak or not to speak? That is the question," he said.

."I think I'm gonna do it," she answered.

"Seriously?"

"You seem surprised." She laughed.

"Yeah. A little. Yesterday, you seemed pretty

stressed about it."

"Still am. In fact, I'm totally freaking out about it."

Thatcher tried to think of something witty to say, to make her laugh and not worry. But he couldn't come up with anything, so he stuck to a generic "What's the worst that could happen?"

Kaeya was silent for a few seconds. "I really don't know, and I'm not sure if I want to find out."

"Just say *I love you* at the end, and it'll all work out."

"Thatcher, that's really not funny anymore, you know."

"Sorry, you're rubbing off on me."

"Oh, please no. I don't think the world could handle another me."

KAEYA

She leaned back on her chair and searched for the words.

The opening paragraph was good, and the second was okay. Now if she could only come up with a good conclusion.

She turned toward the window, where a couple of yellow birds were bopping around on a tiny branch. Had Sam been there, he would have got out his camera and started filming. She smiled as she remembered, and let her heart bleed onto the page.

Sam always noticed the beautiful things, when others walked past them, their eyes glued to their phones.

THATCHER

He'd worn the shirt on the worst day of his life, and now he was wearing it again, proudly. He straightened the neck and looked in the mirror. The stupid-looking shirt had brought him a lot of pain, but it had also given him a voice.

Yes, he'd told himself he wasn't going to wear it anymore. But tonight he needed it, to honor a friend.

He wasn't worried about the logistics. Posting a video blog would be easy. He used to post YouTube book reviews back in junior high, in the days when ten views were amazing. Based on the amount of views his memes were getting, this one would draw a lot more.

After doing a couple of test takes on his laptop, he was ready. He stared into the webcam and began:

> Hey, all. It's me, the Marry Me Martha guy, live and in person. In case you're wondering why I'm stepping out of the memes tonight, it's for a friend, Sam Park. He died yesterday morning in his sleep, and I wanted to do something special to remember him.
> At first I thought of posting a quote. But that didn't seem like enough. Because his friendship was too big for a post, and his loss too painful for words. So I came up with something else.
> I've decided to post my quote tomorrow, in person at Glen Canyon

High. Bring a sign, or a quote, to the quad
at break, and we'll send Sam off right.

As he previewed the clip, he wondered. How many people would show up? And if they did show, would Mr. Blakely freak out about the unplanned event taking place in the quad?

"Whatever," he said as he hit upload. Mr. Blakely owed him one.

23

MONDAY

KAEYA

The quad was usually crowded, but this was insane.
They'd seen Thatcher's video. Definitely.

Kaeya pushed her way through the crowd, her
nightmarishly heavy book bag weighing her down. Was
Thatcher already there? She didn't want him to have to do
this alone.

Standing on the edge of a planter, she saw him.
He was climbing onto a table and lifting a sign above his
head, just like he had two weeks ago. Only this time,
there were no insults, only silence as he grabbed the
crowd's attention.

The Martha Baines T-shirt looked the same as it
did on picture day...but Thatcher looked different. Gone
was the tragic expression, and in its place, strength. He'd
rewritten the narrative. Amazing.

THATCHER

The quote was Helen Keller's.

What we once loved deeply we can never lose
...because it's become a part of us.

He closed his eyes as he raised it over his head.
And when he opened them again, the campus had
changed. The quad had become a collage of iPads, hastily
scribbled quotes, and posters, many of them pointed
upward, as if to let Sam read.

Some skaters held painted skateboards over their
heads, spelling Sam's name.

A group of girls held a long paper banner with a
line from a Tennyson poem, *God's finger touched him,*
and he slept, while the anime club raised a manga-style
poster board with a tribute written in Japanese.

Everywhere he looked, there was color and
language and love. Overwhelmed, Thatcher sat down on
the table and gazed out at the crowd.

Kaeya climbed up and sat next to him. "You did
good, Thatch," she said as she put her hand on his knee.

"Yeah, I figured this place needed a little
remodel," he said as he pulled her close.

"Thatcher, we all needed some remodeling," she
answered.

When the tribute faded, Thatcher was mobbed by
students and teachers. There were a lot of hugs and a lot
of tears as they remembered one of their own...together.

24

KAEYA

The school's orchestra played a shaky version of "In the Arms of the Angels" as students filed into the gym.

"You'll do awesome." Mrs. D smiled as Kaeya climbed the steps to the stage.

But Kaeya wasn't so sure about that. She'd been feeling sick to her stomach all morning. There were a lot of people there, more than she would have guessed.

As she sat down on one of the chairs behind the podium, she noticed Sam's sister in the front row with her two kids, along with some other family members that she didn't recognize. Thatcher was there, sitting behind them in the second row. He was watching with encouraging eyes, and that helped.

When the song was over, the principal stepped up to the podium, and the gym grew silent.

He began by saying something about life, and death, and how we should cherish every moment, but Kaeya wasn't listening.

I can't do this, she obsessed as she watched the side of his mouth move.

With the stress came TS, causing her neck to tic and her folding chair to wobble a little. She stabilized

herself with her foot and reviewed her notes to distract
herself. But she ticked anyway.

I can't do this.

She thought of escaping. It would be easy. She'd
been doing it all year.

But this time her legs wouldn't budge. Because
she was the only one in the entire school who really knew
him. Because Sam's sister was dabbing her eyes with a
tissue. Because the moment was bigger than Tourette's.

The principal was folding his notes now and
placing them in the front pocket of his suit. He was
finished.

She took a deep breath and moved toward the
podium. It was time.

THATCHER

Kaeya adjusted the microphone, cleared her throat, then
stepped away.

Thatcher sat up in his seat. Why was she
stopping?

Then he noticed her face. It was doing that scowl
thing. *Oh no*, he thought as she stepped back up to the
microphone.

"Mama always said that dying was a part of life,"
she began, her voice trembling. "I sure wish it wasn't.
Forrest Gump said that. Sam loved that movie. In fact, he
told me that on the day we met."

She coughed twice, then continued. "I was the
new girl at Glen Canyon. I didn't know anyone here. I
walked into the Gallery, and there he was, typing away

on his laptop like there was no tomorrow."

Kaeya moved away from the mike again, turned her face from the crowd, then returned. "See, S-Sam never...Sam never once..."

Thatcher gripped the sides of his metal folding chair. *Come on, Kaeya.*

Whispers swirled as students obviously wondered what was up. The principal turned towards Mrs. D, who raised her hand as if to say *wait*.

Thatcher watched in horror as Kaeya fumbled with her notes. She was having a full-blown TS attack at the worst possible moment.

"*HA!*" she yelled into the mike, startling the crowd.

Students pointed toward the stage and whispered as Kaeya vocalized again, this time into her arm.

She tried to cough it away, but it wasn't working. The vocalizations were too intense, too obvious to hide.

"Okay, this is awkward," she said as she dropped her notes and backed away from the podium. She was crumbling, right there in front of everyone, and Thatcher felt like racing onto the stage like a Navy SEAL to rescue her.

But she didn't need rescuing. She was moving up to the podium again, rescuing herself. "Sorry if I freaked you guys out," she restarted. "It's just that I have this neurological condition, Tourette syndrome. It makes me, well, do what I just did."

More hand-over-mouth whispers. More feedback from the mike. When the sound died down, Kaeya continued.

"But enough about that. This is about Sam, who knew about my Tourette's, who saw me twitch and yell and contort my face pretty much every day, who would look up from his laptop and smile whenever I'd scream something random into the air. The guy knew how to smile—everyday he would smile."

Kaeya's voice cracked, and she wiped her eyes. "And I'm gonna miss those smiles more than anything, because those smiles were telling me I was okay just the way I was. And it wasn't just me. He accepted everyone like that, with that same smile, with that same *you matter to me* attitude. Not a lot of people can love like that, but Sam did."

The gym was silent as she walked back to her seat, and a slide show began. And as pictures of Sam's life flashed across the giant screen, Thatcher began to weep, for Sam, for Kaeya, for every sorry thing that every person in the room had ever had to put up with in this broken world.

KAEYA

The gym lights turned back on, Mr. Blakely said something, and it was over. All of the hiding. All of the pretending. Everything.

As Kaeya stepped off the stage, she was met by Sam's sister, who gave her a massive hug. The hug set off an avalanche of emotions, and Kaeya began to bawl.

Sam's sister offered her a tissue. "Thanks for being Sam's friend," she said. "And thank you for being you."

The principal was there now to offer his condolences to the Park family, along with other school officials. So Kaeya shook a few more hands and backed away.

Thatcher was waiting patiently at the back of the crowd. When their eyes locked, he gave a little wave. She started to walk over to him but felt a tap on her shoulder.

She turned. It was Kieran, hands in his pockets, head down.

"Hey," he began. "I want to apologize for my momentary loss of sanity. It's just that the whole Tourette's thing took me by surprise. I didn't know how to handle it."

Kaeya recognized the tone. Guilt. "Oh, so you're saying you didn't have a soccer tournament?" She already knew the soccer thing was a lie, but asked anyway.

"I guess we could go out again, for coffee or something...to make it up to you," he continued, his words lacking conviction.

Pity. She didn't have time for it, not anymore. "You don't need to make anything up to me, Kieran," she said. "And anyway, I've been kind of busy lately." She pointed toward Thatcher. He smiled and walked toward them.

Kieran stepped back. "Oh, I'm sorry. I didn't realize you guys were..."

"Together? Um, yeah. It's kind of new."

An awkward silence fell as Kieran stared at the floor. She almost felt sorry for him. Almost.

"Well, nice talking to you, Kieran," she eventually said as she grabbed Thatcher's hand and walked away.

25

THATCHER

Thatcher held the DVD like a holy relic, as if the plastic were a piece of Sam himself. Had he mailed it from the hospital? He must have.

It had come with the afternoon mail, in a yellow envelope. There was a Post-it Note on the case.

Our Movie
Prepare yourself for AMAZEMENT! (ha ha)

Part of him wanted to race inside to watch it, and part of him wanted to put it back in the envelope and scream like he'd seen a ghost. Sam had mailed this. Sam who was no longer here.

Sitting down on the top porch step, he pulled out his phone.

"You won't believe what I'm holding in my hands right now," he said softly.

KAEYA

"Ready?" she asked as she picked up the remote. With

one press of the button, Sam's trailer would begin, his last mark on the world. But it all seemed too big, too final, too much. She couldn't hit play.

"Here, let's press it together," said Thatcher as he put his hand over her thumb and pressed.

The screen went blue for a few seconds. A cool indie song began to play. A title appeared on a wrinkled piece of paper.

This Infinite Ache

She recognized the title, from one of Thatcher's posts, Friday's post. Sam must have been editing in the middle of the night, before his surgery.

The camera moved down a dimly lit staircase, past family pictures on a wall. And as it reached the bottom of the stairs, Sam began to narrate.

> *There's an unfortunate side effect of love,*
> *an infinite ache that keeps us up at night.*

The camera moved through the doors of a kitchen, where a clock displayed the time, 3:30 a.m. Sam's sister was there rocking her sleepy-eyed little girl in the light of the moon. She was singing something about fairies and stars, her soothing tone fitting perfectly with the film's indie soundtrack. As the teary-eyed baby fell asleep, the narration continued.

> *A mother feels it when her baby cries*
> *and she doesn't know why*
> *or when she waves good-bye through a kindergarten*
> *fence.*

The camera then shifted seamlessly to a small room where a soft morning sun poured through an open window. Sam's grandmother was sitting on the edge of her bed, her head bowed. She was praying silently, with tears rolling down her cheeks.

It haunts us when we can't find the words,
when they need a miracle,
but our magic's run out.

Kaeya used the sleeve of her sweatshirt to wipe her eyes just in time to see one of the scenes she'd filmed with Thatcher. It was during one of Sam's perfectionist streaks, when they were stuck on the computer. He must have left the camera running after one of their takes.

Your such a loser...I love you, she typed.
***You're** a grammatical loser, and I*
love you too, he typed back.

Thatcher stared up at her, looked back down at the keyboard, then stared again. And she blushed.

Kaeya didn't remember blushing.

He feels the sting when she touches his arm,
and he wonders if it was on purpose.
And she feels it while waiting
for the phone to ring after a perfect first date.

The music began to wind down as the scene transitioned to a busy airport terminal, where a man, which she assumed was Sam's father, dropped his bags so he could give his wife one last hug.

In every kiss
In every goodbye
It's there, this hollow sting beneath the surface

The song began to fade, along with the scene. And when the screen was fully black, everything grew silent except for Sam's words, his last to the world.

Because love is more than
big screen kisses and happy endings.
It's a glorious mess that reminds us we're alive
And, yeah, it aches.
But it's worth it.
Totally.

THATCHER

They stared at the screen in silence for at least a minute, as if the film, and Sam's life, would somehow go on.

"Oh my gosh, that wasn't the movie we signed up for, was it?" sniffed Kaeya as she leaned her head on his shoulder.

"I guess the dude knew what he was doing after all," he answered as he wiped away his own.

"No, actually, he didn't."

"What?" Thatcher asked, baffled by her last comment.

"I mean, look. The *dude* completely cut out all of

my lines."

He shook his head and smiled. He loved the way she could laugh, even in the rain.

"I mean, I could have won an Oscar or an Emmy or a Grammy or something," she added.

"Um, Grammys are for singing," he explained.

"I know. But I was *that* good," she argued. "They would have given me the Grammy anyway."

"Hey, I'm the one that should be complaining," said Thatcher. "He used one of my quotes without permission!"

"I know. We'll sue him together. A joint lawsuit," she said.

The jokes were stupid, but they laughed anyway, and kept laughing. As they talked about Sam's video and how amazingly incredible it was. As they watched dumb YouTube videos together. As they wondered aloud whether Sam was laughing along.

26

ONE MONTH LATER

KAEYA

The pavement was still wet from a light morning rain. But the clouds—somehow aware of the importance of the event—had cleared away, allowing the sun to paint Paradigm's back lot in a warm orange glow.

"This is so embarrassing." Thatcher laughed as he fiddled with his cell phone camera.

"Hey! You're the one that wanted to post this on your page," she lectured as they stopped under a Parisian-style streetlamp. Going back to Paradigm Studios to finish Sam's movie trailer was her idea, a symbolic gesture to remember the one-month anniversary of his passing.

Thatcher pushed *Record*. It was time.

"What does okay even mean? Is it some lame excuse for failure?" she said. "I want better than okay. I want perfect." She smiled goofily, and Thatcher tried hard not to laugh.

He wrapped her in his left arm while balancing the phone in his right. "Let me show you what perfect feels like," he said.

Then as a warm ray of afternoon sun fell down on them, they kissed...until Kaeya started cracking up.

"What? Are my kisses that bad," he asked.

"I'm sorry. I feel so stupid." She laughed.

Thatcher pulled down his phone. "You *do* know Sam was messing with us, right?" he said as he stared down at the screen.

"I know—that's what makes the lines so funny."

The security guard checked his watch as if to tell them that their time was running out. After a full month of e-mails and pleading phone calls, they'd been given ten minutes, and *only* ten minutes, on the lot. They needed to hurry up.

"So did you get it?" she asked.

"Yup, there it is," exclaimed Thatcher as the clip began to play. "The walk, the hug, the kiss. Perfect.""Sam's happy ending," she said, satisfied.

Thatcher kissed her on the cheek. She would have kissed him back, but the security guard assigned to babysit them was pulling up in his golf cart. They hopped in the back, and the cart took off. Barring any movie monster attacks, the ride to the parking lot would take about seven minutes. She wished it were longer.

She looped her arms around Thatcher's and watched as back lot streets whizzed by. "Hey, you," she whispered.

"What?" he asked as he leaned his head on top of hers.

"I love you," she said with a yawn.

Thatcher broke away from her grip and stared.

"Wait a second," he said with a sheepish grin. "Don't you mean *You're such a loser—I love you* or *Your hair's a mess—I love you*?"

"Nope, just I love you," she said as she snuggled closer.

Thatcher's face grew serious. He looked out at the buildings for a second, then back into Kaeya's eyes. "Well then, I love you too," he said.

And there it was, Thatcher's first *I love you*, with no shooting stars, or fireworks, or miraculous rainbows in its wake. And even though it was simple, it was beautiful and true and perfect...because that *I love you* was all she'd ever needed.

THATCHER

Thatcher took the Martha Baines T-shirt out to the backyard and threw it in the trash. With his YouTube channel going so well, he'd decided to ditch the memes altogether.

On his way back, he passed the kitchen window where he saw Mom and Scout playing Candyland. Scout was laughing about something, and Mom was pretending to be angry.

Scout spotted him through the window and waved. And in that tiny moment, he knew for sure.

It was going to be a good day.

ABOUT THE AUTHOR

Once upon a time, author Alex Marestaing wrote a random letter to the Walt Disney Company asking if they needed any creative help. Fortunately, Disney had mercy on his embarrassing attempt to break into the publishing scene and gave him his first writing job. A lot has happened since then, including four novels, a beautiful wife, three kids, two cats, an extremely mellow dog, an honorable mention at the London Book Festival, a stint covering soccer in Europe and the U.S., and fun freelance work for companies such as Lego, Thomas Nelson/Harper Collins and The Los Angeles Times. Oh yeah, he also speaks at conferences around the country giving writers advice such as "Writing letters to random companies isn't always such a bad idea"

www. Alexmarestaingbooks.com

Thanks for reading! Please add a short review on Amazon and let us know what you thought!

Lightning Source UK Ltd.
Milton Keynes UK
UKHW020639191220
375447UK00013B/3119